Coping with death

Coping with Death

Shasta Gaughen, *Book Editor*

Daniel Leone, *President*
Bonnie Szumski, *Publisher*
Scott Barbour, *Managing Editor*
Brenda Stalcup, *Series Editor*

Contemporary Issues
Companion

GREENHAVEN
PRESS®

THOMSON
GALE

San Diego • Detroit • New York • San Francisco • Cleveland
New Haven, Conn. • Waterville, Maine • London • Munich

For more information, contact
Greenhaven Press
27500 Drake Rd.
Farmington Hills, MI 48331-3535
Or you can visit our Internet site at http://www.gale.com

LIBRARY OF CONGRESS CATALOGING-IN-PUBLICATION DATA

Coping with death / Shasta Gaughen, book editor.
p. cm. — (Contemporary issues companion)
Includes bibliographical references and index.
ISBN 0-7377-1521-9 (pbk. : alk. paper) — ISBN 0-7377-1520-0 (lib. : alk. paper)
1. Death—Psychological aspects. 2. Grief. 3. Loss (Psychology). I. Gaughen, Shasta. II. Series.
BF789.D4 C665 2003
155.9'37—dc21 2002035394

Printed in the United States of America

Contents

Foreword

In the news, on the streets, and in neighborhoods, individuals are confronted with a variety of social problems. Such problems may affect people directly: A young woman may struggle with depression, suspect a friend of having bulimia, or watch a loved one battle cancer. And even the issues that do not directly affect her private life—such as religious cults, domestic violence, or legalized gambling—still impact the larger society in which she lives. Discovering and analyzing the complexities of issues that encompass communal and societal realms as well as the world of personal experience is a valuable educational goal in the modern world.

Effectively addressing social problems requires familiarity with a constantly changing stream of data. Becoming well informed about today's controversies is an intricate process that often involves reading myriad primary and secondary sources, analyzing political debates, weighing various experts' opinions—even listening to firsthand accounts of those directly affected by the issue. For students and general observers, this can be a daunting task because of the sheer volume of information available in books, periodicals, on the evening news, and on the Internet. Researching the consequences of legalized gambling, for example, might entail sifting through congressional testimony on gambling's societal effects, examining private studies on Indian gaming, perusing numerous websites devoted to Internet betting, and reading essays written by lottery winners as well as interviews with recovering compulsive gamblers. Obtaining valuable information can be time-consuming—since it often requires researchers to pore over numerous documents and commentaries before discovering a source relevant to their particular investigation.

Greenhaven's Contemporary Issues Companion series seeks to assist this process of research by providing readers with useful and pertinent information about today's complex issues. Each volume in this anthology series focuses on a topic of current interest, presenting informative and thought-provoking selections written from a wide variety of viewpoints. The readings selected by the editors include such diverse sources as personal accounts and case studies, pertinent factual and statistical articles, and relevant commentaries and overviews. This diversity of sources and views, found in every Contemporary Issues Companion, offers readers a broad perspective in one convenient volume.

In addition, each title in the Contemporary Issues Companion series is designed especially for young adults. The selections included in every volume are chosen for their accessibility and are expertly edited in consideration of both the reading and comprehension levels of the audience. The structure of the anthologies also enhances accessibility. An introductory essay places each issue in context and provides helpful facts such as historical background or current statistics and legislation that pertain to the topic. The chapters that follow organize the material and focus on specific aspects of the book's topic. Every essay is introduced by a brief summary of its main points and biographical information about the author. These summaries aid in comprehension and can also serve to direct readers to material of immediate interest and need. Finally, a comprehensive index allows readers to efficiently scan and locate content.

The Contemporary Issues Companion series is an ideal launching point for research on a particular topic. Each anthology in the series is composed of readings taken from an extensive gamut of resources, including periodicals, newspapers, books, government documents, the publications of private and public organizations, and Internet websites. In these volumes, readers will find factual support suitable for use in reports, debates, speeches, and research papers. The anthologies also facilitate further research, featuring a book and periodical bibliography and a list of organizations to contact for additional information.

A perfect resource for both students and the general reader, Greenhaven's Contemporary Issues Companion series is sure to be a valued source of current, readable information on social problems that interest young adults. It is the editors' hope that readers will find the Contemporary Issues Companion series useful as a starting point to formulate their own opinions about and answers to the complex issues of the present day.

Introduction

The way in which death is handled in the United States has changed dramatically since the beginning of the twentieth century. At that time, the elderly and those with terminal illnesses usually died at home, surrounded by their families. Now it is much more common for people to die in hospitals, often after drastic medical procedures have been implemented in attempts to prolong their lives. According to grief counselor Amy L. Florian, Americans no longer consider death and bereavement as normal and natural processes. Instead, she asserts, the American method of coping with death is to ignore it. Americans usually do not want to think or talk about death, Florian finds, nor do they want to deal with the emotions associated with grief. They tend to assume that those who have experienced the loss of a loved one will be able to quickly overcome their grief through publicly sanctioned rituals such as funerals. However, for most people, coping with death is a long and arduous task. This realization has led psychologists, psychiatrists, social workers, and other grief and bereavement specialists to develop a variety of ways to help people handle emotions of grief and loss.

In 1969, psychiatrist Elisabeth Kübler-Ross published *On Death and Dying,* a book that has had a tremendous influence on views toward death in the United States. Kübler-Ross pointed out that changes in the quality and availability of health care meant that people were living longer than ever before. Death during infancy and childhood had been greatly reduced due to vaccinations and antibiotics, as well as improved health education and access to medical treatment. Adults were less likely to die before reaching old age due to the advent of additional medical innovations, such as chemotherapy and advanced surgical techniques. As a result, more and more people were dying at an older age.

In addition, Kübler-Ross noted, death was increasingly becoming separated from the home environment, instead taking place in medical settings such as hospitals and long-term care facilities. Family members were no longer the primary caregivers for the dying, and it became less likely that most Americans would witness the gradual, natural death of a loved one. "Old-fashioned" death customs that had allowed dying individuals to wrap up their affairs and say goodbye to friends and family were being circumvented by complicated medical procedures designed to prolong life indefinitely. When death finally did occur, the body was whisked away to be embalmed and preserved in as lifelike a state as possible, whereas in the past, it had been common for family members to take an active role in preparing the body for burial. Kübler-Ross stated that these dramatic changes were "ultimately responsible for the increased fear of death, the rising number of emotional problems, and the greater need for understanding of and coping with the problems of death and dying."

Kübler-Ross suggested that a better understanding of the grieving process would allow health care practitioners to better help their patients face their own mortality or the deaths of loved ones. Drawing on her own experiences working with the terminally ill, she proposed that grief progresses through five stages: denial, anger, bargaining, depression, and acceptance. The denial stage is characterized by a refusal to believe bad news, such as a diagnosis of a terminal illness. When denial can no longer be maintained, people frequently become angry that such a terrible thing has happened to them. They feel resentful toward those who are not suffering as they are. As the reality of their situation continues to sink in, however, they attempt to bargain with God or fate, trying to make a deal that will result in a miracle. By promising to behave in a certain manner or to complete certain tasks, they hope to make things "the way they were before." As people realize that nothing can be done to change their situation, bargaining gives way to depression. The terminally ill often become depressed as they contemplate everything they are leaving behind, while those who have lost a loved one may feel guilt, regret, and a sense of deep loss. Finally, once all the previous stages of grief are exhausted, people come to terms with the reality of their situation and begin to accept it.

While Kübler-Ross's work on death and dying was, and continues to be, very influential, bereavement experts today believe that coping with death is not quite so simple as the five stages make it sound. For example, they point out that not everyone grieves in the same way: Children deal with loss much differently than adults do, and men and women have distinct ways of experiencing bereavement. Another vital factor to bear in mind is cultural diversity. In the United States, with its rich mix of cultures from around the world, death and loss are approached in a wide variety of ways. For example, writes psychologist Richard R. Ellis, Orthodox Jews do not permit cremation, yet Conservative and Reform Jews both accept cremation as an alternative to burial. Hmong immigrants from Southeast Asia, Ellis reports, have a traditional prohibition against allowing an individual to die in the house of someone who is not a relative. Many Native Americans of California still perform a ceremony in which all the possessions of the deceased are burned. With such disparate customs concerning death in the United States, bereavement experts stress that health care providers and other professionals must avoid being ethnocentric or assuming that individuals share their own values and traditions in coping with loss.

Experts on death and dying are also attempting to change the way in which people die. Instead of continuing the medicalization of death, they advocate a return to the original, customary practice of allowing people to die at home. Dying in a hospital is often a stressful and frightening experience not only for the patient, but for family members and friends as well. Doctors sometimes resort to extreme life-saving measures against the wishes of family members, leaving them to feel helpless as medical decisions concerning their loved one are removed from their hands. However, physician Myles N. Sheehan maintains that death does not have to be an overwhelming, painful affair. With proper planning, he writes, it is possible to "die well." A terminally ill patient can draw up legal documents asserting exactly what measures should or should not be taken to artificially prolong his or her life. A good death also includes addressing the spiritual dimensions of dying.

All of these principles are embodied in the practice of hospice care. Hospice is specifically intended to help patients with terminal illnesses ease their way into death, while at the same time reducing the burden of caregivers, who are frequently family members. Hospice care enables many terminally ill individuals to stay at home by providing periodic visits from hospice nurses who check on the patient's condition, administer medications and pain relief, and support the patient's family. Other individuals who are too ill to remain at home can be cared for in hospice facilities that strive to create a natural, noninstitutional environment. Hospice care is rapidly becoming a popular alternative to the hospitalization of terminally ill patients.

Despite these recent efforts by bereavement experts and health care professionals to alleviate the concerns of the terminally ill and their loved ones, most Americans are still reluctant to deal with the realities of death and grief. The prospect of dying is not easy for anyone to face, whether they are dying themselves or experiencing the death of a loved one. Yet it is certain that every person will be touched by death and loss at some point in life. The selections included in *Coping with Death: Contemporary Issues Companion* provide a timely and relevant overview of many important aspects of this topic, including planning for the medical and legal aspects of death, dealing with emotions of loss and grief, specific concerns that arise with different types of death, and vital issues in biomedical ethics such as pain management and the debate over assisted suicide.

CHAPTER 1

THE NATURE OF DEATH: AN OVERVIEW

The Evolutionary Purpose of Death

Cedric Mims

Cedric Mims spent twenty years as a professor of microbiology at Guys Hospital Medical School in London, England. In the following excerpt from his book *When We Die: The Science, Culture, and Rituals of Death,* Mims discusses the scientific reasons for the death of organisms. Species must continually evolve in order to adapt to changes in the earth's climate, he explains. In order for evolution to occur, Mims states, there must be competition between organisms, with those that are best suited to a certain environment surviving to pass on their genes to future generations. Death is therefore a crucial component for natural selection and evolution, which otherwise could not take place, he concludes. However, Mims notes that advances in genetic research may someday give humans the power to manipulate their own evolution.

In the body cells are always dying. Blood cells, cells in the skin, those lining the intestines: all are either shed like leaves or degenerate and die. A white blood cell lives for only a few days, and each day we lose millions of cells from our skin and intestines. The fine white dust that you pick up on your finger when you run it over a shelf or other surface consists mostly of dead skin cells, and during a lifetime each of us sheds about 18 kg of skin. The live, naked cells lining the intestines suffer continual physical damage, and are shed after a few days. To replace all these lost cells and keep the body intact, other cells are constantly dividing. Cell death is therefore the natural state of affairs, and 'In the midst of life we are in death.' That passage from the service for the burial of the dead in the Book of Common Prayer takes on a biological meaning.

The Death of Cells

You could say that these cells don't have to die, and that nature could have arranged for them to live much longer. But at the skin surface and in the intestine the inevitable mechanical damage is best met by

Cedric Mims, *When We Die: The Science, Culture, and Rituals of Death*. New York: St. Martin's Press, 1998.

continually shedding cells and replacing them with new ones. And the white blood cells, armed with powerful chemical weapons for use against invading microbes, need to be regularly dismantled and replaced by new ones. It is a common belief that cells in the test tube go on multiplying for ever. But the fact is that no cell can manage more than about sixty divisions. After that, the cell ages and dies. A few types of cell, like nerve cells or heart muscle cells, stay as they are throughout life, all the time recreating themselves as old molecules are replaced by new ones, but not actually dividing.

The reasons why cells have to die becomes more obvious when we consider the development of the embryo. During this period the growing organs are always having to be remodelled and reshaped. Certain structures have to be demolished and cells destroyed. Our tail and our gill slits, for instance, present in the early embryo as we recapitulate our origin from primitive vertebrates, must be altered and diminished at later stages in development. In the same way the tadpole's tail is disposed of as the tadpole turns into a frog. As these events unfold, cells have to be killed off. A great deal of destruction accompanies the process of construction. Accordingly, to take care of these needs, all cells have a special 'autodestruct' or suicide program built into them. It can be switched on as required, and is an essential resource during development, and in certain infections when cell suicide is the best strategy for defeating the attack. It is called 'apoptosis.'

The Necessity of Death: Nature's Strategy

Life is a process of constant change. All living things must reproduce and multiply, and when they die their offspring take their place. But the places are limited. The opportunities, or in modern jargon the ecological niches, are not infinite. There is a limited amount of room on the earth. This means competition, and the best fitted ones are going to survive and out-reproduce the others. This is how evolution works. Without death, the world would soon fill up with whatever creatures were present at the time, and there would be no more change, no more evolution. Without death, a single cell, after dividing each day for many weeks, would have produced hundreds of tons of cells and these would rapidly cover the surface of the earth. Nature is so prolific that death has to take a hand, even at the level of the elephant. If a female elephant bore six young during her lifetime and they all survived and reproduced at the same rate, then after 700 years the descendants of a single pair would number about 18 million. Hence the struggle for existence. Death is necessary. To die and leave the stage is the way of nature. It was put simply by the French moralist Michel de Montaigne (1533–92) in his essay 'To Study Philosophy is to Learn to Die': 'Give place to others, as others have given place to you!'

Death takes other things besides the individual at the end of life and the cells in the developing embryo. Certain objects are needed at one time but can be discarded when they have served their purpose. The placenta is doomed to die after the birth of the offspring, and is usually eaten by the mother (except in human beings). The umbilical cord soon dries up and dies, leaving its mark. Adam, strictly speaking, should be represented without a navel.

Death Ensures Evolutionary Change

Why, we might ask, has nature chosen the strategy of death, the strategy of billions of short lifetimes, rather than some other basis for life? It is because this is the only way to ensure change, which, together with competition, is the driving force of evolution. The ultimate reason for sex is that it is a method for mixing together the genes of different individuals. It increases the variety of gene mixtures, and gives evolution something to work on.

The best way of looking at it is to remember that your germ cells (eggs, sperm) are fundamentally different from the rest of you. These cells, or a few of them at least, will outlive you, surviving after the egg has been fertilized and then dividing to form a new individual, your offspring. All the rest of you, all your somatic (bodily) organs and cells, die when you die. It is your DNA, your genes in the eggs and the sperm, that survive in your descendants. This is the pathway for changes in genes being handed down through the generations and allowing evolution. You and your body are no more than a device by which the germ cells ensure their immortality. To put it the other way round, your body sacrifices itself so that the germ cells can live on. Nature cares about the survival of your DNA rather than the survival of you yourself. The distinction between the immortal line of germ cells (the *germa*) and the mortal rest of the body *(soma)* was made more than a hundred years ago and is a useful one.

Why Immortality Would Raise Problems

One other possibility would have been for nature to have produced superorganisms that never aged or died. But agelessness would have serious drawbacks. First, it would have made it impossible to achieve the drastic transformations in living creatures over millions of years that were needed to adapt to changing conditions. Animals and plants have had to undergo fundamental changes in response to alterations in climate, food, predators and so on. They did it by producing new individuals (offspring) at regular intervals, each generation showing slightly altered features. This allowed for change. The penalty for failure to change and adapt was death. Second, it would mean that as the old individuals accumulated there would soon have been no room for future generations. Third, there are daunting biological problems in designing an immortal.

One of these biological problems concerns DNA. Our genes have to put up with constant low-grade bombardment and irradiation damage which comes from rocks and from outer space. All cells make occasional mistakes when they are making a second copy of their own DNA in preparation for division. These changes in DNA are called mutations, and they are nearly all harmful. Initially, most of the changes are corrected or repaired, but as cells get older they are less able to carry out the repairs. The DNA abnormalities accumulate and cell functions are interfered with. This has a lot to do with ageing and cell senescence. How would the immortals get round this problem? An immortal species, if ever it arose, would be staking its existence on a single solution to the problem of survival: its solution. Assuming that thousands of other species were still around, these would still be undergoing the relentless change and adaptation that has been the stuff of life ever since it began. The immortals would have to watch out and keep these other species in their place, not permitting any developments that might threaten their supremacy. They would also have to control their own numbers at an optimal level for the environment. They would have to look after their own evolution, and in doing so would be distorting the archetypal rules of the game. They would have replaced nature.

Manipulating Human Evolution

Am I giving a description of the human species at some distant future time? Once all the secrets of DNA are solved and we know exactly how to make whatever we want, there will—theoretically—be no limits on what we can do to manipulate human development. We have probably already exempted ourselves from the ancient rules of nature, because the 'unfit' now survive; and little is known about what changes this is making in our gene pool. Once we had the capacity to modify, change, even improve our genes in the laboratory, we could take over our evolution—as we have already taken over the evolution of dogs, cats, cattle and other domestic animals. It seems unlikely that our present characteristics, the ones that evolution selected out as best for a hunter-gatherer life 100,000 years ago, for a life of uncertainty, famine and disease, would be appropriate for human life in the distant future.

Contemplation of such possibilities arouses a host of ancient fears. What opportunities for madmen, for despotic rulers, for mad or at least unethical, scientists! Words like 'cloning' add to the foreboding, and we regard this picture of the future with dismay. But it will almost certainly come to pass, and will probably not be so bad as many fear. For the apprehensive, there is the reassuring thought that checks and brakes will still exist in the form of the old-fashioned, uniquely human qualities like wisdom, common sense and, perhaps most old-fashioned of all, lovingkindness.

Modern Perspectives on Death and Dying

Michael M. Uhlmann

Americans are very reluctant to deal with the fact that someday they will die, contends Michael M. Uhlmann in the following selection. He explains that death in the United States has changed dramatically from the past, when many people died young, most individuals died at home, and the majority of Americans were Christians who understood death to be the passage to the afterlife. Today, in contrast, he states, Americans enjoy a long life expectancy, and most die in hospitals or nursing homes. However, Uhlmann maintains, the weakening of traditional Christian values in American society has led many people to turn to New Age spiritualism to try to understand their mortality, while others hope to keep death at bay through futuristic technologies such as cloning or genetic manipulation. Uhlmann is a senior fellow at the Ethics and Public Policy Center in Washington, D.C., and the author of *Last Rights? Assisted Suicide and Euthanasia Debated.*

Although Americans live longer, healthier lives than their ancestors did—or perhaps because of this—they seem to be less easy with the prospect of their own mortality. As Evelyn Waugh observed in *The Loved One*, his bitingly satirical novel on contemporary funerary practices, we sometimes go to bizarre and comical lengths to avoid thinking about the one irreducibly predictable fact of human existence: one day we shall die.

Philippe Aries, the noted student of the rituals of death and dying, argues that modern culture makes death "invisible and unreal." In a culture that has taken great pains to banish the idea of evil, he says,

> a heavy silence has fallen over the subject of death. When this silence is broken . . . it is to reduce death to the insignificance of an ordinary event that is mentioned with feigned indifference. Either way, the result is the same: Neither the individual nor the community is strong enough to recognize the existence of death.

Michael M. Uhlmann, "How Do We Die?" *World & I*, vol. 13, July 1998, pp. 22–27.

Dealing with Death

In short, we seek to banish the terror of death by the simple device of not dealing with it until we absolutely have to; and when we are forced to do so, we try to insulate ourselves from its true significance. In the meantime, the fewer reminders we have of its presence, the better.

Strive though we may to ignore or postpone our date with death, sooner or later it comes. The most obvious fact about death today, however, is that on average it's coming later rather than sooner. This means that we're more likely to die of "natural causes," the general deterioration of the body as it reaches the end of its apparent biological course.

At the other end of the life span, violent death—homicide, suicide, and accident—is a far more common occurrence. Indeed, violence claims the lives of two-thirds of all those who die between the ages of 1 and 19. Of the 2.3 million American deaths in 1996, nearly two-thirds were attributable to three causes: heart disease (733,834), cancer (544,278), and stroke (160,431). Thereafter, the percentages fall off rapidly.

The next seven leading causes of death aggregate only a fourth of the total for the first three, and the tenth (chronic liver disease and cirrhosis) accounts for only 1.5 percent of the whole. Although men and women share heart disease and cancer as the two leading causes of death, men are more than twice as likely to die in accidents.

Other differences between the sexes: HIV infection, suicide, and homicide are seventh, eighth, and tenth, respectively, on the list for men, but none of the three makes the women's top-10 list. On the other hand, women are more likely to die from kidney disease, blood poisoning, and Alzheimer's disease, largely because they tend to live longer.

Where People Die

Significantly, nearly 80 percent of all deaths now occur in a health-care facility of some sort—about three-fourths of these in hospitals, the remainder in nursing homes. At the turn of the nineteenth century, when health insurance and terminal-care facilities were virtually unknown, most people died at home, often from infectious disease. (As late as 1918, an estimated 675,000 Americans died during a deadly influenza pandemic that may have claimed as many as 50 million victims worldwide.)

The new locus of death underscores not only the increasingly medicalized manner of our dying but the fact that we tend to die when older. By living to a ripe old age, we increase our chances of dying in an institutional setting, attended by health-care personnel and sustained till the end through the marvels of chemistry and technology.

Few health statistics are so dramatic as the change in life expectancy during the twentieth century. Baby Sally, born in 1900, could expect to live but 49 years. If she were born today, she could expect to see 80, and her brother would live well into his 70s.

One measure of increased longevity is the sharp decline in childhood mortality. Children born in 1900 had only an 80 percent chance of making it to age 15; today, their chances are nearly 100 percent. Moreover, couples with three children in 1900 could expect that one of their youngsters would die before reaching maturity. Today, those odds have declined more than eightfold.

And our longevity promises to continue, albeit at a somewhat slower pace: Social Security Administration actuaries estimated in 1994 that over the next 50 years, life expectancy would increase from 72.4 to 77.5 years for males and from 79 to 83.4 years for females. By 2030, the number of people 65 or older is predicted to rise to 64 million, or slightly more than 20 percent of the population. Between now and midcentury, we will likely see a fivefold increase in octogenarians.

This historically unprecedented longevity curve has many causes: the abundance of our economy; better housing, sanitation, and nutrition; and the explosion in medical knowledge and health care. But the laurel wreath may go to antibiotics, which have tamed or conquered numerous pathogens that cut down our ancestors by the millions before they reached old age.

Indeed, the problem today is that by overusing antibiotics, we may expose ourselves to the new risk of potentially fatal, drug-resistant microbes. It would be a savage irony indeed if the age of science were to end on so ignominious a note.

Changing Attitudes

Whatever the future may hold, these remarkable changes in the facts of life—and death—appear to have occasioned an equally dramatic change in our attitudes about dying. Although Americans are far more religious than other citizens of the Western world, clearly religion has a weaker claim on our loyalties than it had for our parents and grandparents.

The Christian understanding of life and death, which has dominated the Western ethos for the past 2,000 years, still retains a strong hold in American life. But it has been weakened by a culture that now celebrates material comfort and the claims of autonomous individualism.

Whereas life was once commonly understood as a divine gift and death as an opportunity to be reunited with God in heaven (or damned to hell for one's sins), a new attitude has taken root—one composed of almost equal parts of pride, cynicism, pagan mysticism, and faith that science may one day postpone, perhaps even indefinitely, our appointment with the grim reaper.

The old dispensation began with belief in divine governance of the universe, the new with an affirmation of man's right to control his own destiny. The tension between them is tellingly displayed on the shelves of today's bookstores.

There one can certainly confirm a renewed interest in the literature of Christian salvation, but one is also powerfully struck by the fascination with spiritualism, pagan religious rituals, and a seemingly endless supply of "self-help" titles that promise to relieve our anxieties. This same amalgam appears in microcosm in works dealing with death and dying, which seem to multiply by the month.

Many of these bespeak a Christian understanding, but just as many, if not more, advance New Age religious beliefs and assorted pop-psychology prescriptions for happiness, along with pseudoscientific information about prolonging life and postponing death. You will also find various how-to manuals for achieving a "dignified" death, by which is chiefly meant the ability to exercise control over the time and manner of its occurrence.

This mix is hardly surprising. An age unsure of its beliefs will search for meaning everywhere it can. As British author G.K. Chesterton famously remarked, a man who no longer believes in God does not believe in nothing; he will believe in anything. And in this peculiarly materialistic and comfortable age, when science threatens to rob life of much of its mystery, books that reintroduce an element of the mystical are bound to multiply, even as we gobble up works that promise to slow or even reverse the aging process.

Perhaps we suffer the same temptation that once tormented the unfortunate Ponce de Leon in his feckless search for a fountain of youth. There is, however, this difference: Whereas he understood the fountain to be a miraculous departure from nature, we expect it to be revealed through the marvels of modern science.

Although the study of aging has become something of a cottage industry in university and—significantly—commercial laboratories, we're still not quite sure what causes the body to age. Some argue that we're genetically preprogrammed to decay within an allotted time span, and that's that. Other scientists incline more toward what might be called a wear-and-tear theory.

The Life and Death of Cells

Cell biologists can provide evidence for both theories and a host of others in between. Why some cells cease to multiply is no less mysterious than why others insist on multiplying endlessly, but in either event the damage done by both can be deadly. Whatever one's favorite theory of bodily decomposition, for the moment at least, we are sure of two things: On average, women's bodies will outlive men's (although the gap is narrowing) and, give or take change, 80 years appears to be the allotted human life span (although the ceiling is rising).

But whether we live to be 60, 80, or 100, the central question remains what we will do when the fact of our own mortality can no longer be avoided. Some scholars, like cultural anthropologist Ernest Becker, have argued that twentieth-century society is characterized by nothing so much as "the denial of death"—the avoidance of discussion about death and the consequent suppression of grief.

This modern disposition, says Aries, arises from the secularization of society and the growth of self-conscious individualism. The former reinforces materialistic accounts of existence that preclude thought of an afterlife; the latter strengthens our sense of control and entitlement. When the power of science and medicine is added to this mix, we are less inclined to accommodate ourselves to a divine plan and more disposed to insist that we are rightly masters of our own fate.

"Wild" vs. "Tame" Death

But as the scene of death shifts from home to hospital, our sense of control must seem very weak indeed in the presence of modern medical technology and the bureaucratic indifference of many health-care institutions. Under such circumstances, one's death can be reduced to an anonymous event or even a mere statistic. Once denuded of religious meaning and isolated from the affairs of a living community, death can become not only a very private affair but a frightening one as well.

Aries calls this "wild" death, in contrast to the "tame" death that characterized the profoundly Christian culture of the Middle Ages. Dying was then part of a complicated social and religious ritual performed before the entire community. When his end approached, a dying man notified family, friends, and priest, apologized for the wrongs he had done to others, confessed his sins, received the Eucharist, and took to his bed to await death.

Many from the community, young and old alike, participated in the bedside deathwatch until the end came. Death was thus a public and profoundly religious activity that united the living with the dying and the fact of this world with the promise of the next. Death was "tamed" precisely because it was openly acknowledged and understood by all as but the natural extension of life into the next world. As the Catholic funeral ritual to this day puts it, life is not ended, only changed.

By contrast, death in the late twentieth century is seen as a kind of meddlesome interloper disrupting a pleasant party. As novelist Somerset Maugham once put it, "Dying is a very dull, dreary affair. And my advice to you is to have nothing whatsoever to do with it."

While it is probably too much to describe this sentiment as a "denial of death," we are certainly inclined to keep death at a respectful distance on the out-of-sight, out-of-mind principle. And when it does intrude, many place more faith in material comfort and scientific remedies than in religious wisdom.

In his old age, Maugham desperately sought and received exotic medical treatment to enhance his fading youthful vigor. It did no good. Others have sought solace in the increasingly popular remedy of cosmetic surgery, and for the truly imaginative there's always "cryonics," by which they hope to be frozen and preserved for a future time when science can accommodate their revival. For yet others, genetic manipulation, or even full-scale cloning, is a consummation devoutly to be wished.

One or more of these "remedies" may someday do the trick. In the meantime, however, some assert that we should have a legal right to direct the circumstances of our death. Witness, for example, the growing interest in assisted suicide. Jack Kevorkian, the sometime Michigan pathologist who by his own account has "assisted" more than 100 persons to their deaths, has survived three jury trials without a scratch. Clearly, he is seen by many as a kind of savior. His appeal seems to be that if our deaths can't be postponed or avoided, they can at least be kept within our power to control.

But if doctors follow Kevorkian's lead in bowing to patient autonomy, they will have to invent an entirely new philosophy to govern their dealings with patients. The doctor-patient relationship as we have traditionally known it was formed by the principles of the Hippocratic oath, which anthropologist Margaret Mead once described as the distinctive feature of Western medicine.

Since the early days of the Christian West, the Hippocratic tradition has bound doctors to use their unique power and knowledge for the good of the patient—a good that cannot include killing him. The debate over assisted suicide, however, goes beyond the narrow question of how doctors and patients deal with one another. It may ultimately decide whether Western civilization can withstand the assault of the modern temperament. In the conflict between those who believe that the rules of life and death are divinely ordained and those who insist that our lives are ours to dispose of as we will, there is precious little room for compromise.

The Scientific Search for the Soul

John Elvin

Many people who have been resuscitated from clinical death describe what are called near-death experiences (NDEs), which tend to share common features such as traveling down a tunnel toward a bright light. In the following selection, *Insight on the News* staff writer John Elvin takes a look at scientists who have begun studying the NDE phenomenon. According to the author, the researchers involved in one NDE study concluded that the mind can exist independently of the brain and may continue to be conscious after bodily death. In fact, Elvin explains, a number of scientists who began their research as skeptics of NDEs have become advocates of their existence. However, he reports, these supporters often abandon a scientific approach to NDEs, instead focusing on them as spiritual phenomena. Skeptics contend that NDEs can be explained logically as delusions that arise from the effects of anesthesia and oxygen deprivation on the brain, Elvin notes.

What awaits us beyond death's door? That ancient question generally is considered a speculative one, a religious or spiritual inquiry suited for mystics, visionaries and seers. But today the same science that brashly is delving into the secrets of life also is probing the mysteries of death. The highly credentialed authors of a recent British study of near-death experiences (NDEs), heralded in the popular press as the first "scientific" study in the field, say they seem to have discovered a "mind" separate from the brain. Whether it is in fact a soul remains a matter of speculation.

Peter Fenwick, coauthor of the study and consultant neuropsychiatrist to several leading British medical institutions, says, "If the mind and brain can be independent, then it raises questions about the continuation of consciousness after death. It also raises the question about a spiritual component to humans and about a meaningful universe with a purpose rather than a random universe."

John Elvin, "In Search of the Soul," *Insight on the News*, vol. 17, September 10, 2001, pp. 10–15.

Definitions vary but the literature on these matters indicates the classic NDE results from severe trauma and could be described as a transcendental "trip" out of ordinary reality into a special realm where peace and joy are experienced intensely. Closely related and often preceding the NDE is the out-of-body experience (OBE), where a brain-dead or cardiac-arrested patient often believes he or she is present in the operating room as a conscious double, observing events—usually from above.

Fenwick says of the OBE that unconscious, technically dead patients "know what's going on around them in a way which is very detailed and suggests that the mind may have separated from the brain." The British study was conducted among serious heart-attack victims because those persons have lost consciousness immediately and gone into a clinical state of death—no respiration, no cardiac output and a nonfunctioning brain stem.

Evidence for a Soul?

Does this independent mind that seems to survive death have any relation to the religious concept of a soul? Fenwick, asked this question in an interview, responded: "We'd be getting close to that."

The problem for scientists is that the area they are attempting to study, like experiencing religious conversion or other spiritual and mystical sorts of enlightenment, is subjective and defies hard, cold, rational inquiry. Those who undergo NDEs often are barely capable of describing the adventure. Words fail them, and often they are reluctant to attempt a description for fear of being thought crazy.

Browsing the appropriate shelf in almost any bookstore provides evidence of the fringe nature of the core experience, as one encounters offerings including *Embraced by the Light, Saved by the Light, Transformed by the Light, One With the Light* and *Beyond the Light.* It is reported that 35 to 40 percent of patients who come close to dying report having had NDEs. Their stories abound in books and in the popular press.

Louis Farrakhan, the recently reclusive leader of the Nation of Islam and a famous firebrand, attributes his new kinder, gentler message of unity and peace to an NDE during treatment for complications related to prostate cancer. Singer Della Reese, star of the TV series *Touched by an Angel* and an ordained minister, says she encountered angels while at death's door following a burst brain aneurysm. Others mentioned, at least anecdotally, include former U.S.S.R. president Mikhail Gorbachev, comedian Roseanne Barr, director George Lucas, actress Debra Winger and actor Donald Sutherland.

Studying Near-Death Experiences

Contrary to the British "first-ever" claim, scientific studies seeking evidence of life after death actually commenced in the United States some years ago. There is a long track record of the scientific method being applied to this phenomenon, says Carlos Alvarado, a psychologist serving as a program director for the Parapsychology Foundation headquartered in New York City. Alvarado, whose considerable body of published work includes a recent article on this subject in the *Journal of Nervous and Mental Disease*, tells *Insight on the News (Insight)* that researchers in psychology and psychiatry have developed all kinds of methods for studying phenomena that are by nature very subjective—dreams, hallucinations and thought processes that we don't know how to measure physically.

How are such scientific studies conducted? An example might be a study where subjects are interviewed and then their descriptions related to their oxygen levels while in the NDE state. That would yield certain facts useful from a scientific perspective. But, Alvarado acknowledges, the evidence thus far doesn't allow us to take the leap into a claim of scientific findings regarding an afterlife. It still is speculation, but it's a developing field. What we need now is more systematic research and large-scale studies. The British study, he points out, was very small.

The fact that there are common or core experiences—classically, the perception of moving toward a great white light—is well-established. Fenwick and his colleagues cite other common threads: peace and calm, going through a tunnel into another dimension or realm, meeting a being of light and going into a garden. Variations on these themes are found in written and oral traditions as old as human memory.

Also, many who returned from near death believe they experienced a presentation—a "life review"—and others recall fusing with a universal intelligence or consciousness. It is not uncommon that survivors express anger or grief at having been "brought back." Most survivors lose their fear of death, and many lose interest in financial gain and other aspects of the conventional "successful" lifestyle. Many others feel a general sense of love for other people and are convinced that they have been given special knowledge of the afterlife. As a result of the experience, the lives of most are changed dramatically in a very positive way.

One of the more popular lecturers and writers on the subject is Betty J. Eadie, a mother of eight who tells a touching tale of meeting and talking with Jesus when, at age 31, she died during heart surgery. Eadie, whose early writing on the subject has been disparaged by some colleagues as promotional material for the Mormon church, lectures these days as a generic Christian with New Age overtones. She says she saw angels rushing to answer the prayers of the living. She describes physical handicaps, desperate lives and tragic deaths as aspects of a progression of the spirit. Eadie has a compelling tale, but it is hardly scientific evidence capable of independent confirmation.

From Science to Spirituality

Perhaps the most fascinating finding in *Insight*'s survey of NDE studies is that the physicians, psychiatrists, psychologists and other researchers involved often cross over from their roots in hard science to become bearers of a spiritual, cosmic message. Melvin Morse, for example, links the NDE to a "God spot" in the brain that allows access to timeless and universal realities. Once a total skeptic, Morse now is recognized as one of the leading researchers in the field. He began to take another look when a child who had been through an NDE confronted the researcher's doubts with the words: "Don't worry, Dr. Morse, heaven is fun!"

Morse has added substantially to the scientific credibility of NDE research through extensive controlled studies, but his research has put him on a new path. Today he is less concerned with the hard science of his field and far more likely to tell listeners about a spiritual path where "love is all there is."

The same is true of many other highly credentialed researchers now specializing in NDE and related areas. Raymond Moody, a doctor of medicine and philosophy who has authored several best-selling books, is credited with coining the phrase "near-death experience" back in the 1970s. He is described as "the first medical professional to do work in this area." Today he devotes a lot of his time to teaching others how to evoke the spirits of departed loved ones. Perhaps his most controversial contribution to the field is the "psychomanteum," a re-creation of the mirror-gazing process used by ancient Greeks to communicate with spirits. He claims to have introduced more than 300 people to the process and says many of them believe they contacted a dead relative or other spirit in the mirror.

Among other pioneers in the field is Bruce Greyson of the department of psychiatric medicine at the University of Virginia in Charlottesville, editor of the *Journal of Near-Death Studies*. He also has evolved as a spiritual enthusiast and recently told an interviewer: "What happens [to those who have had an NDE] is that when they lose their fear of death, they also lose their fear of living life to the fullest because they're not afraid of taking chances anymore. They're not afraid of dying. So they actually get more interested in life and enjoy it much more than they did before."

NDEs Change People's Lives

Most of those engaged in NDE research acknowledge the work of psychology professor Kenneth Ring as pivotal in moving their field out of the fringe and into mainstream science. Ring, the author of *Lessons From the Light* and other books on the subject, is noted for his meticulous, scientifically structured research. But from that foundation he also has ventured beyond the realm of conventional science. When we die, he writes, we go through a second birth, which may be even more difficult than the first, and leave the world we know for another that transcends anything we can conceive. There we discover, finally, what it is to be fully alive and filled with a radiant joy beyond the realm of happiness. He is the founder of one of the major organizations in the field, the International Association of Near-Death Studies (IANDS).

Denise Wade, international spokeswoman for IANDS, had her NDE in 1977. "When I learned that others reported similar experiences, I at first wondered if we are all dreaming the same dream," she tells *Insight.* Wade lives in Munich, Germany, but was in the United States recently during an annual IANDS conference. She contends that her experience wasn't a dream. "It really happened; it changed my life," she tells *Insight.*

In Wade's view, trying to make a hard science of the study of these experiences probably is a waste of time. "It's anecdotal. You cannot even prove by hard science that there's a God. I'm more interested in the positive, transforming nature of the experience. The public that is interested in NDEs isn't asking for numbers; they want to know the nature of their mission on Earth."

Wade emphasizes: "One is granted the near-death experience from suffering." She says her experience resulted when she was nearly beaten to death and required an emergency operation that lasted seven-and-one-half hours. She recalls traversing a silver cord toward heaven. "I met spiritual friends," she recalls, whom she believes guided her through a life review. She came to believe that "we absolutely do have angelic presences that are always, always, watching over us." Her story is told in the book, *The Case for Heaven.* What's the lesson in a nutshell? "It's all about love," she says.

Scientific Explanations for NDEs

Are there no disbelievers? Armies of them, no doubt, but their books and seminars have not seized the public imagination. The average enthusiast, conventional neuroscientists lament, is not overly interested in discussions of brain chemistry and the effects of anesthetics and lack of oxygen on the billions of neural cells working to maintain the balance of the human guidance system. Just as some researchers contend that dreams simply are the effort of the brain to sort and file the day's activities, so it is suggested that NDEs are just the way the brain processes the approach of death.

The most prominent critic of ethereal interpretations of NDEs is Susan Blackmore, senior lecturer in psychology at the University of the West of England. Author of *Dying to Live,* she favors the effects of oxygen depletion as an explanation for the broad similarities of the anecdotes, and she terms the reported experiences of life after death an "illusion" based on beliefs and unsupported by physics, biology or psychology. As to the transformative results of this experience, Blackmore says that people tend to become less selfish and more concerned about others after having survived a brush with death. "We are all biological organisms, evolved in fascinating ways for no purpose at all and with no end in mind," she says.

Blackmore suggests that OBEs are constructed from fragments of memory. The out-of-body view from above, she says, occurs because that's how memory functions. "Try to remember the last time you went to a pub or walked along the seashore," she writes, adding that your view of the scene no doubt will be from above. She also observes that hearing is the last sense to go as we lose consciousness, and anyone who has listened intently to a storyteller knows how the mind constructs images to go with the spoken word. So some memories may be constructs based, for instance, on operating-room conversations. Blackmore believes that "trips" similar to NDEs can occur under a variety of circumstances and recounts one of her own induced while smoking marijuana.

Do all experiencers have joyful adventures and return feeling warm and fuzzy? In a research paper published by the *Christian Research Journal* a few years ago, the author surveyed books covering the "dark side" of these events. The report notes that some NDEs are indeed "hellish" and "terrifying" and that survivors tend to repress memories of them. One book title says much: *Beyond the Darkness: My Near Death Journey to the Edge of Hell.* The author, Angia Fenimore, tells of her experiences resulting from a suicide attempt.

P.M.H. Atwater, a longtime researcher and author who has experienced the near-death phenomenon and also has made a careful study of the encounters of others, reports that about 15 percent of adults and 3 percent of children enter "a threatening void or stark limbo or hellish purgatory," sometimes including "hauntings" from the past. She suggests that these experiences often are based on the person's expectations and psychological predisposition toward guilt, fear and the anticipation of punishment.

Continuing the Search for a Soul

Where can science possibly go with this subject? Fenwick, coauthor of the British study, suggests that the next studies should include setting up secret targets in the operating room that could only be seen from the ceiling. That's the vantage point of most NDEs. Survivors then could be asked to describe what they had seen.

The reaction among religious leaders to what might be regarded as playing games with the soul could be the subject of another entire article. In general, religious leaders take a we-told-you-so attitude toward recent scientific findings in the area. In response to the British study, the bishop of Basingstoke, the Right Rev. Geoffrey Powell, a member of the Church of England's Doctrine Commission, commented: "These near-death experiences counter the materialist view that we are nothing more than computers made of meat."

The mystery of death is a subject of intense human curiosity and always has been an area as open to conjuring charlatans and witch doctors as to systematic theologians and devout mystics. But, as this survey has shown, it increasingly is viewed as a legitimate area for mainstream scientific inquiry, stopping just short of government subsidy. It will be interesting to see how science deals with the seductive nature of this issue, especially in view of the way in which many who in recent years have approached it clinically have found themselves giving religious testimony.

The great leap of modern science into the search for the soul is a leap, all right—one that began at the very wellsprings of human musing and yearning.

The Possibility of Reincarnation

Allen Abel

Belief in reincarnation is central to many cultures around the globe, as Canadian journalist and broadcaster Allen Abel reports. In the following selection, Abel focuses on the work of anthropologist Antonia Mills, who has spent more than thirty years researching reincarnation beliefs among several Native American nations in British Columbia, Canada. Mills and some of her fellow researchers have come to the conclusion that reincarnation may indeed be a fact, Abel writes. While there is as of yet no actual scientific proof for reincarnation, he states, scholarly research strongly supports the probability that there is life before birth. If scientists eventually prove that reincarnation does occur, Abel explains, it will mean drastically rethinking the way Western science views the world.

In the folds of the Skeena River, in the womb of the forest tribes, a boy is born into the Wolf House clan of the Gitksan Indians. While pregnant, his mother has flown through vivid dreams in which a high chief, dead for decades, vows to return as her son. Now, when the baby comes, there are precise indentations on the rims of his ears, matching the initiation scars of the headman.

A man named John is shot. Two years later, a baby is born in his settlement with round wounds on the abdomen. A man falls off a fishing boat and drowns, and his grandson, conceived soon after, screams at the sight of water. Or a toddler visits her grandparents' house for the first time and points and says, "That's my chair."

Researching Reincarnation

For more than thirty years, a woman out of Iowa with a Harvard Ph.D. has been living and working among the peoples of northern B.C., and dressing herself in their articles of faith. Among the natives' strongest beliefs—the one that has become Antonia Mills's focus and fixation—is that the soul survives after bodily death to be refashioned in the form of a child.

Despite her professional detachment and the rigour of scholarly doubt, these decades on the frontiers of the cedar forests and the human psyche have not left Dr. Mills unaltered. She and other acade-

Allen Abel, "Soul Survivors," *Saturday Night*, vol. 113, September 1998, pp. 33–34.

mic researchers into reincarnation have vetted thousands of hauntingly veritable cases in dozens of cultures from Canada to Calcutta. What they suggest is that—possibly, but not yet provably—somewhere in our genetic code lies the schema of immortality.

"What is memory?" she muses, as I spend a few days with her in Prince George, where she is Associate Professor of First Nations Studies at the handsome new University of Northern British Columbia (UNBC). "Can memory survive without a brain? Is it not a kind of energy—a motivational force seeking to come back?

"The Indians say, 'This baby is so-and-so come back.' I wonder, 'What does this mean to them?' And, 'Could this really be the way things work for all human beings?'

"To them, human beings do come back. They don't expect that everyone will have clear memories of who they were, but everyone is impacted by who they have been. These memories become diluted by having spent various and sundry amounts of time in a realm they now describe as 'heaven.'

"I don't expect the answers to be simple. What is important at this point is simply asking the questions. If physical forms are some kind of condensation of energy, are we dealing with forms of energy we are not capable of measuring and understanding at this stage of our development?"

An Expert on Reincarnation

There was no Department of Paranormal Studies at Harvard in the early sixties. Antonia Mills had been raised in Iowa City, the daughter of a professor of American civilization. She would have followed her father's path to Yale, but Yale didn't accept "girls." So she went to Radcliffe, where women had just begun being granted Harvard degrees.

She graduated in anthropology, magna cum laude with highest honours, then followed her first husband, a doctoral candidate, to work with the Beaver Indians in the Peace River country of B.C. The landscape of Canada's native heritage enfolded her and has never let her go.

"The Beaver Indians were the ones who first really made me think about reincarnation," she says. "They kept raising the issue over and over. It was so foreign to me—it didn't fit with the concepts you were taught in university courses. Nothing at Harvard prepared me for this. They didn't teach us to ask questions about the survival of the human soul.

"I wrote to my parents. My dad said he had read the Bhagavad-Gita and concluded that if there is life after death, then there must be life before birth. I took that as his permission to pursue the subject."

In Vancouver, she was introduced to Dr. Ian Stevenson, the Montrealer and McGill University man whose methodical, sceptical exploration of hundreds of cases suggestive of reincarnation in Alaska, India, and all points between has rendered him the paramount expert on the phenomenon and—much to his displeasure—a hero to legions of Shirley MacLaine screwballs. Stevenson gave Mills some articles to read and some leads to pursue and, later, brought her to the University of Virginia with funding for still more studies of death before life.

"Her work is of high quality, but because of limited funds I was unable to offer her tenure," Dr. Stevenson says by phone from Charlottesville. "In Virginia, the attitude toward us and our work has been uneven and at times quite hostile."

Neither Stevenson nor Mills—with fifty years of case studies between them—is prepared to trumpet the headline news that reincarnation is fact. Both have repeatedly turned down Oprah Winfrey and shun the popular press. Dr. Mills has never found a hint of past-life knowledge in her four children or herself.

"Many years ago, I sketched out the criteria for what would be the 'perfect case,'" says Dr. Stevenson, who will turn eighty this Hallowe'en. "Since then, I've presented thousands of cases, all of which have flaws when considered individually, but taken collectively, the inference is, in my opinion, quite strong. It becomes a matter of increasing probability, not finding one perfect case."

Belief in Rebirth

At Dr. Mills's lakeside A-frame, with eagles in the trees and hummingbirds at the feeder, I am introduced to Sarah Layton, chief of the Dark House clan of the Witsuwit'en nation. Europeans labelled her people "Carrier Indians," for their custom of a widow's carrying the ashes of her husband for a year after his death. This they no longer do.

The chief, like Dr. Mills, is careful in her speech and shy with strangers probing a belief system condemned by European Christians as voodoo heresy. (The Catholic Church abolished belief in reincarnation at the Second Nicene Council in 787, calculating that communicants would pray more fervently if they believed they had only one go-round at redemption.)

A central figure in Mrs. Layton's childhood was her maternal grandmother, Christine. The old woman predicted that Sarah would enjoy a long life and that she would become the head of her clan. "You are the one who will look after us," the old woman said. And this has come true.

"Grandmother used to dream a lot, out on the trapline," the chief says. "She always said that she saw in her dreams that I was someone born again. She said I was her Uncle Alexander, the old chief of my house. He had come back first as my brother, who died when he was ten, before I was born. When I was born, they said I was Alexander come back again.

"When you're young, you don't want to be told that you're someone reborn. I didn't believe it then. Now, I'm sixty-eight. I believe it. When I go back to the land, the voices from the old times are as loud as sirens in my ears."

To the Gitksan, the Witsuwit'en, and other nations of the Northwest Coast—the Kwakiutl, the Tsimshian, the Tlingit, the Haida—reincarnation is a cardinal tenet of the workings of the world. (Grandmother Christine has "come back" as a girl, now twelve and given the same name, in Moricetown, B.C.) The implication is deeply resonant: we are our ancestors. Yet each tribe holds a different view of the process of rebirth.

Sometimes, it is revealed to the expectant mother or a relative in what anthropologists call an "announcing dream." Or, before death, a person will predict where he will be reborn and by what scars or birthmarks he will be known. In some traditions, the dead return to their own clan, usually as their own great-grandchildren. In rare cases, toddlers declare their previous identities as soon as they learn to speak, or an infant cries uncontrollably until soothed by a hat or blanket belonging to its former self. No-one claims to be Tutankhamen or Marie Antoinette.

The Implications of Reincarnation

"What if reincarnation is a fact?" I ask Dr. Mills in her office at UNBC, and give her the weekend to think it over.

"I think people would treat children with more respect," she says on Monday. "And for people who believe in reincarnation, it makes one's attitude toward death less fearful."

To Antonia Mills, thirty years of probing such cases has led to intriguing possibilities: that past-life memories may influence the codes in our nucleic acids; or that our cultural precepts influence how the universe unfolds. Either explanation—if it could be "verified"—would blast Western science to smithereens.

"Think of Einstein's theory of relativity," she says. "The theory was true before it was proved—the universe was operating according to those laws long before they were understood by human beings. But look at how those laws have been used and abused by human beings since Einstein wrote them down. Look at India and Pakistan setting off nuclear bombs.

"If reincarnation works, then it has been working without our understanding how it operates. If it is true, it should not be necessary for us to believe in it for it to occur. But if we are able to prove that it occurs, the question becomes what do we do with that understanding?

"One of the things that are happening is a demonstration that thought has an influence on reality. When we talk about the different cultural perceptions of reincarnation, we're talking about human thoughts and human desires. In the Buddhist conception of reincarnation, it's desire that brings you back. But whose desire—the dead person's, or his community's?

"If reincarnation is explaining these phenomena, then the issue becomes, in anyone's world, what does it mean to be Uncle Alexander?"

Searching for the Afterlife

Peter Stanford

When considering the fact that one day they will die, most people find consolation in the idea of heaven and life after death, according to Peter Stanford. However, he explains, contemporary mainstream religions do not dwell on elaborate beliefs about the hereafter, leaving an emotional void that individuals must try to fill. Some people seek solace in spiritualism, Stanford writes, including séances held by psychic mediums in which participants attempt to contact the spirits of their departed loved ones. Recounting his own experiences at a séance, Stanford casts doubt on the validity of spiritualism, but he asserts that such beliefs are mostly harmless and help people to find some comfort and reassurance about what happens after death. Stanford is the author of *Heaven: A Traveller's Guide to the Undiscovered Country*.

Sir Arthur Conan Doyle stares out reassuringly from his portrait above the fireplace. The tilt of his head is slightly defiant, no doubt the product of enduring years of ridicule in his crusade in defence of spiritualism—the idea that you can communicate with the "other side". It was a trend so fashionable between the mid-19th century and the end of the First World War that even Queen Victoria had a go at it.

Sir Arthur, whose comical handlebar moustache makes me smile, looks down upon 12 people in the Conan Doyle Room at the British Spiritualist Association headquarters in Belgrave Square, central London.

They are an odd bunch, fidgeting in their seats and doing everything possible to avoid meeting anyone else's gaze. When I break the taboo and stare at the man in the front row, he responds by bolting for the exit.

A palpable embarrassment fills the air, as if we are sitting in the waiting room of a sexually transmitted diseases clinic. Instead, we've paid our £4 and are expecting the duty medium—there's one on offer every day at 3.30 and 7.30—to appear. Not literally. At least, I hope not. I'm jumpy enough already.

Peter Stanford, "Knock Knock. Who's There? A Dead Man's Spirit," *New Statesman*, vol. 131, April 8, 2002, pp. 32–33.

Life After Death

I'm feeling oddly uncomfortable about the prospect of going to a seance. It will be my first; and I had planned to remain a virgin. Then, prompted by the death of my Catholic mother, I started researching a book about the heaven she believed in, and felt it would have been absurd not to road-test the alternatives, including Conan Doyle's contention that we can contact those beyond the grave and be given proof positive of a glorious hereafter.

"All agree," he wrote in 1918 of his conversations with the dead, "that passing is usually both easy and painless and followed by an enormous reaction of peace and ease. The individual finds himself in a spirit body which is the exact counterpart of his old one, save that all disease, weakness or deformity has passed from it. This body stands or floats beside the old body and is conscious both of it and the surrounding people. At this moment the dead man is nearer to matter than he will ever be again."

It might prove an enticing message for some, but I fear an implied threat in this dark room.

The exit door is close to my seat and suddenly looks very inviting. My unusually clammy palms, linked defensively in front of my body, reveal my own mixed motives. I haven't, for instance, brought a notebook—just in case I find myself being guided by a spirit into automatic writing. The rational, 21st-century part of me tells me it is stuff and nonsense, but, to be honest, I am terrified of putting it to the test, lest it be proved to have some value. Logically, I must at some level believe in the claims.

Attitudes About Heaven

My reaction is a good metaphor for contemporary attitudes to heaven. History, science and psychology point to it being a collective delusion, designed to take the edge off mortality and soften the random blows of fate in this life. On one level, most of us sign up to this randomness, and treat heaven as some quaint medieval antique, nice to look at in paintings in art galleries, but utterly irrelevant to our lives. Yet when push comes to shove and the specialist tells us the test results are bad, the heaven that we have so far scorned suddenly becomes our next best hope. At which point, many find they have some core belief in a greater power and the trappings that go with it.

I imply no criticism. Heaven offers consolation by the bucket load, but then so, potentially, does spiritualism—though at least heaven requires some investment by way of imagination, faith or religious practice. Spiritualism, by contrast, requires only £4. Mark Twain memorably damned it as "a mean little 10 cent heaven". Allowing for inflation, that may be what I'm about to get.

At which stage, Joan, the duty medium, sweeps in. In my mind, I am expecting Madame Arcati, as played by Margaret Rutherford for

Noel Coward. Instead, I get a Welsh housewife in her mid-fifties in a plain blue dress and neat white jacket. She might be about to do a cookery demonstration. She takes her place at what looks disconcertingly like an altar at the front of the room and launches into a brief and understandably partisan introduction to spiritualism. What catches my attention is less her bald statement that its claims have been scientifically proven, even though history shows unequivocally that they haven't, but rather her effort to place spiritualism firmly within the Christian tradition. Hers is a sanitised version of the long and uneasy relationship between the two. She even rounds off by leading us in a group prayer to God to encourage us all to be open.

While she does not use the word "heaven", preferring to talk of "those who live in the spirit" inhabiting "the astral plane", she nevertheless conjures up a heady cocktail of all the best audience-pleasing details of heaven's history—the promise of reunion with loved ones, the hum of constant activity ("You can even learn new skills there," she chimes, like an employment counsellor), the physical beauty of both the landscape and its inhabitants.

What she doesn't borrow from Christianity, however, is the difficult bit: the idea of judgement in death. That would mean some of her audience may be searching for loved ones who may not have made the cut at the Pearly Gates. Unlike them, we are all going to be satisfied in the next hour, it seems.

Trying to Talk to the Dead

Joan explains that her own spirit guide has arrived at her shoulder. She even starts a little, as if he or she has just goosed her. Her eyes begin spinning like a roulette wheel. Someone's lucky number is about to come up. We all become tense.

"I want to come to the lady sitting at the back in the beautiful necklace." Joan is pointing elsewhere. The rest of the room breathes a collective sigh of relief. "I have a tall African gentleman here for you. Can you accept him?" The woman looks around confused, as if the said gentleman is about to appear through the curtains behind the makeshift altar like a guest on *This is Your Life*. "He has a special concern for you."

The woman is still straining to see him. Joan doesn't hang about waiting for her to catch up. "Can you hold on to that, think about it later, ask others?" The woman nods, utterly disorientated. "You've a birthday coming up." The woman has at last cottoned on. It's her granddaughter's birthday next month, she tells us all. It's a result.

It hasn't been an auspicious start, but Joan now alights on much more receptive raw material, a well-scrubbed young woman sitting eagerly in the front row. "I'm seeing the word healer above your head." The woman nods eagerly. There follows much talk of alternative remedies, health foods, t'ai chi, yoga and a long-lost grandfather who is playing the role of guardian angel. The blond head is bobbing enthusiastically at every take.

It is the high point of the session. Joan scores very few more hits as she darts around the room, falling victim often to her own stereotypes. Two Afro-Caribbean women are told that there is a spirit from the West Indies calling them, but they insist that they have lived in Birmingham for generations. An Indian-looking man is being contacted by someone sitting in a restaurant.

By the time Joan gets to me, I am not frightened. There is a father figure calling me from New England. My dad back in Birkenhead got his passport just two years ago at the age of 80, so she is way off there. Then she tries to read the words above my head and, after toying with technology—I've a big head—and teacher, she plumps for actor. In a narrow sense, she is right. My audition next week, she says, will go well and I will get the part that will make my name.

Yet there is something in the way she gives me my "messages" that means, instead of saying "actually, completely wrong", I find myself muttering "well, yes, sort of". In part, it's my middle-class anxiety about making a scene. Yet it is also that I would be easy game for any second-hand car dealer: Joan's technique is, I recognise, classic salesmanship. Never take no for an answer. Roll on relentlessly until you force your hearer to say yes.

The Appeal of Spiritualism

But what exactly is Joan selling, and what is the profit? The second question is easier. A dozen people at £4 a head is £50 a hour. Then there is her final pitch, having given us all a taster, when she offers individual, in-depth sessions. The blond girl has her chequebook out at once. That will be another £50.

Yet it is still such a small-scale operation that I cannot quite believe it can be worth the effort unless the motivations are more complex. Transparent as Joan's deception is, there is no obvious malice in her, and I am quite happy to believe that her play-acting is born out of a genuine desire to help the walking wounded who turn up each day. With a touch of the frustrated actress thrown in. She may even delude herself that she is really hearing messages. The only damage done comes in terms of unfulfilled expectations.

Hence the continuing appeal of a seance—or, for that matter, spiritualism's more recent descendant, the Near Death Experience movement, where 13 million people in the United States claim to have had a peek at heaven while drifting in and out of life. Mainstream religion, long the arch promoter of heaven as either a perfect garden or a mystical union with the Almighty, has gone remarkably quiet about the hereafter. Pope John Paul II has described it only once during his long reign, and then, in July 1999, in bland terms as "a state of being" after death. The heaven that once fired imaginations, that seemed to promise an eternal reward for the injustices and sufferings of life, is no longer mentioned. Yet we still yearn for it. A recent Gallup poll had 70 per cent signing up to some kind of afterlife—not because it makes sense in our secular and scientific age, but because human beings are the only animals who have to live with the knowledge that they will die one day, and the promise of heaven allows for some comfort.

And who knows, after all, if there is anything in it? Joan certainly struck a chord with one member of her audience. The blond head is just turning happily out through the door when I spot, swinging from her hand, a white plastic bag—which was no doubt at her feet in the front row of the room—emblazoned with the logo of an alternative medicine shop.

CHAPTER 2

PREPARING FOR DEATH

Facing Death with True Dignity

Christina M. Puchalski

Christina M. Puchalski is an assistant professor of internal medicine and the director of the George Washington Institute for Spirituality and Health at the George Washington University School of Medicine in Washington, D.C. In the following selection, Puchalski explains that people with terminal illnesses often have many spiritual questions that need to be answered. However, she observes, because the medical emphasis is on fighting to prevent death for as long as possible, both doctors and patients frequently overlook spiritual issues. In the author's opinion, addressing and meeting the spiritual needs of the dying is an essential step in the process of helping them come to terms with death, yet it is too often neglected. Puchalski relates her experiences with a dying friend that led her to understand the importance of this process. Providing support to dying people on their spiritual journey allows them to face death with dignity and to die at peace, she concludes.

Jim is a 35-year-old gentleman with AIDS. He has two children with whom he is very close. He is dying. Jim called me the other day because he said he felt death was coming soon. He knew that because his frail body no longer carries his clothes the way it used to. He almost did not recognize the face he tried to shave each morning. The sunken eyes lacked that sparkle of life as they peeked out beyond the prominent bony orbits. Every step has been an enormous effort and every breath a labored exhalation.

"I am not who I used to be," he said. "My children clean the house, cook the meals, and nurse me. They are just kids, and I can't be a parent anymore. I have no energy to give. My son is angry at me because he thinks I have given up. I don't think so. I just think it is my time to go."

As I listened to Jim's feelings, his anxieties about leaving the people he loves, mixed with fleeting seconds of peaceful resolve that this is the way of nature, the way of God, I couldn't help but wonder was there one more fight Jim could win with his illness? Was his son right? Could I encourage him to hang on for just a few more months?

Christina M. Puchalski, "Facing Death with True Dignity," *World & I*, vol. 13, July 1998, pp. 34–39.

What About Spirituality?

One key concern of dying patients that needs to be supported is their spirituality. The need for attentiveness to the spiritual concerns of patients has been recognized by many authors. The term spirituality has been used in different ways by different authors. A broad, inclusive definition: Spirituality is that which gives meaning to one's life and draws one to transcend oneself.

Spirituality is a broader concept than religion, although that is one expression of spirituality. Other expressions include prayer, meditation, interactions with others or nature, and relationship with God or a higher power. Spirituality has been cited as integral to the dying person's achievement of the developmental task of transcendence and important for health-care providers to recognize and foster. According to Sally Leighton, writing in "When Mortality Calls, Don't Hang Up," "The physician will do better to be close by to tune in carefully on what may be transpiring spiritually, both in order to comfort the dying and to broaden his or her own understanding of life at its ending."

Some spiritual questions confront each dying person. Is there purpose to his life as he suffers, and can he transcend his suffering and see something or someone beyond that? Is he at peace, hopeful, or in despair? What nourishes his personal sense of value: prayer, religious commitment, personal faith, relationship with others? Do his beliefs help him cope with anxiety about death, pain, and achieving peace?

Saint Therese of Lisieux, a nineteenth-century Carmelite nun, observed of the sisters in her community whose deaths she had witnessed:

> It was without effort that the dying passed on to a better life, and immediately after their death an expression of joy and peace covered their faces and gave the impression almost that they were only asleep. Surely this was true because, after the image of the world has passed away, they will awaken to enjoy eternally the delights.

Therese and her sisters had a profound faith in God and the afterlife. They nourished this faith with prayer. Death was a transition to union with God; as their time drew near, they prepared for it spiritually and hence died in peace. She also had the insight to think about death early in life: "The friends we had there were too worldly; they knew too well how to ally the joys of this earth. . . . They didn't think about death enough, and yet death had paid its visit to a great number of those whom I knew, the young, the rich, the happy!"

Fighting Against Death

What a contrast to our present society. We focus on youth, on looking young, acting young, having aggressive medical treatment to the very last possible moment. Only in the last days of life do we think about the possibility of death. Advances in technology have enabled us to prolong and extend life.

Not all cases should be treated aggressively, however. There comes a time in the course of any illness when cure is no longer an option. In many cases, the techniques used to prolong life actually prolong the dying process, often with increased suffering or loss of dignity.

The Study to Understand Prognosis and Preferences for Outcomes and Risks of Treatments (SUPPORT), conducted by five major medical centers, showed that the majority of U.S. deaths are in hospital settings with frequent use of ventilator support, artificial feedings, and inadequate pain control and anxiety management.

In encouraging people to fight to the end, we neglect to give them the opportunity to bring closure to their lives; to complete unfinished goals; to forgive those they had conflicts with, to be forgiven; to make peace with themselves, with God; to say good-bye; and to die with dignity.

I was honored to be able to walk the journey with Fr. Peter Roberts, a Carmelite priest, as he prepared for his death. Pete had metastatic pancreatic cancer. As we talked about cancer and death, his hand trembled in mine, his voice quivered as he held back tears; he was afraid. His will to continue living was so strong, he grasped for any miraculous explanation that could fulfill his will.

Accepting God's Will

Yet deep within, he understood that it was God's will, not his, that would prevail. Pete's life had not been easy. He faced many challenges that often weighed him down and made it difficult to go on. The turning point for him came when he acknowledged his alcoholism and sought help with the support of his community.

He learned that he was powerless, which was not an admission of defeat but a giving up of the illusion of self-sufficiency. He often said, "God's will, not mine, that is why I am sober and alive today." And so, 25 years later, when he faced the greatest challenge any of us will ever face, he simply turned to God and asked for His help and accepted what God had in store for him.

A few days after our initial conversation regarding his diagnosis, Pete let me know he had decided not to have any chemotherapy. Laughing, he said, "I don't have a wife to go home and vomit for, so I'll just take whatever happens." Underneath that surface humor he so often exhibited was a gentle resolve to accept his dying. This is not to say that once he had made this decision it was instantly a peaceful one.

The first two months were filled with anxieties about dying: Will there be intolerable pain? Would he suffocate? Will he be so helpless that he won't be able to take care of his basic necessities? His theology was challenged. The rigors of adherence to rules were his way of life for 70 years. Now, some of those rules frightened him. Would he go to hell? Had he lived a good enough life as a Christian, a priest, and a brother, as a son and a friend? The judgmental God who had held him in check most of his life and, to some degree, brought him security was closer at hand.

Making Peace with God

Pete was scared. Was this the God he had relied on all his sober life—the forgiving God, the loving God? That God was harder for Pete to understand. What about his friends, family, and community: Would old squabbles be forgotten and old hurts be mended? Pete sat and cried as he spoke of several men in the religious community to whom he felt especially close.

Could he let go? Would he miss them so much that he would hold on longer? Would he really be missed after he died? Would he be remembered? How? I too was scared. I felt the pang of impending separation and wondered if I would be able to handle his permanent physical absence. I was used to his jokes and words of encouragement when I had difficult days. I looked forward to his sermons, because I knew he would make me laugh and remember to take myself a little less seriously. And laughter is healing.

There wasn't a conversation we had, even in the midst of his suffering at the end, where we didn't share at least a few moments of humor. That was what kept Pete going. Pete had also lived his whole life preparing for his eventual death and meeting God, so this time was not a shock but a conclusion to a life's journey.

My own acceptance of his eventual death came when he gave me his books, all inscribed carefully in multicolored ink. (Pete underlined passages of his books in different-colored ink for emphasis as he was learning.) Initially, I regarded the books as a loan; it was easier at some level to pretend that he might recover. Each day, I'd glance at his books on my bookshelf and gradually accepted that he would die soon.

Letting Go

Pete's initial struggle with sadness and anxiety gradually gave way to increasing inner peace and contentment. Pete had decided to make his last months on earth his "final help-out" as he called it. "I want to show the men in my community, my family and friends, how to die well." He wanted to let us see that it wasn't something to dread and fear but rather something to look forward to at a deep spiritual level.

While often he felt a profound sadness and anxiety about leaving, he never forgot about being a presence of gratitude to those around him. One day, a few weeks before he died, I walked into his room, a simple one with minimal amenities. He sat up in bed, gaunt, panting with each breath. Such penetrating sadness came over me; he looked so frail, both weak and in pain. He looked up at me and said, "I am so grateful. I have a wonderful community, family, and friends who have all been so good to me. What a blessed life I have had! I am so grateful for it all."

From behind the ashen skin and tired, drawn eyes came a radiance of joy and peace. There was physical pain and disability, but Pete had transcended that. He had put to rest all the conflicts of his past and all his insecurities and fears. The judgmental God was no longer in center stage. He truly saw God's goodness and grace in all around him and felt at peace in letting go.

His final day on earth was a miraculous one. He was surrounded by the men of his community, by his brother Bill, his sister Polly, and me. We held him, propped up pillows for him, gave him medication to relieve his pain, and prayed with him. His spirit gradually left amid singing and praying and love. We chanted the song "Jesus, Remember Me When We Come Into Your Kingdom" as Pete died. There was no suffering, no pain, no suffocation. Pete died in peace. And as Saint Therese had noticed of her sisters' deaths, with a look of joy and contentment.

What the Dying Need

People who are dying need time to make peace not only with death but also with life. And those of us who are not imminently dying need to face the possibilities of our eventual deaths and live life accordingly. Wayne Muller says in *Touching the Divine:*

> There are times in all of our lives when we are forced to reach deep into ourselves to feel the truth of our real nature. For each of us there comes a moment when we can no longer live our lives by accident. Life throws us into questions that some of us refuse to ask until we are confronted by death or some tragedy in our lives.
>
> What do I know to be most deeply true? What do I love and have I loved well? Who do I believe myself to be and what have I placed on the center of the altar of my life? Where do I belong? What will people find in the ashes of my incarnation when this is all over? How shall I live my life knowing that I will die? And what is my gift to the family of the earth?

Remembering, assessing, searching for meaning, forgiving, reconciling, loving, and hoping are all part of the spiritual journey especially active during the time of dying. It is critical that we allow people who are dying the time to go through this important journey.

Spiritual support is essential in the care of the dying. We need to help foster hope, love, and contentment with their lives in the final days of living. We need to provide an environment where people can be still, pray, laugh, cry, hold, and be held as they are dying.

I don't think I will try to coach Jim on for another win with his illness. I will hold his hand, listen to his fears, his hopes and beliefs, give him the time to bring closure to his life, listen to his stories from the past and dreams for his children after he is gone. And I will support him as he gets ready to die.

Making End-of-Life Medical Decisions

Thomas A. Preston

In the following selection, Thomas A. Preston advises that every person should prepare for the possibility that he or she will have to make difficult decisions about medical care at the end of life. Planning ahead for these decisions, Preston asserts, is a difficult but necessary process in order to ensure a painless death. He addresses several different areas that should be considered, including preparing advance directives for medical decisions, authorizing another person to make medical decisions on the patient's behalf in event of incapacitation, and discussing arrangements for hospice care, aggressive pain management, and the use of heroic life-saving measures with the primary physicians. If these measures are taken, the author concludes, dying should be a peaceful process. A professor of medicine at the University of Washington in Seattle, Preston is the author of several articles and books on medical issues, including *Final Victory: Taking Charge of the Last Stages of Life, Facing Death on Your Own Terms.*

Although medical technology saves the lives of many and is able to prolong life for most of us, we are now in an era of having to deal with an undesirable side effect—prolonged dying. The same technology that adds months or years to patients with otherwise fatal diseases can also extend suffering during the last phases of life. Whereas people with terminal illnesses used to die relatively quickly of pneumonia or heart attacks, the dying process is now extended with operations, multiple rounds of chemotherapy or other treatments that do not cure but only prolong dying.

All too often these new forms of techno-dying mean increased suffering. Although a majority of Americans would prefer to die in peace at home, about 70 percent die in medical institutions and about 40 percent spend at least 10 days in an intensive care unit at the end of life. Worse yet, a majority of dying patients experience severe, undertreated pain in the last stages of dying.

Modern medicine has become sort of a Faustian bargain—we want

Thomas A. Preston, "Dying Your Way," *Total Health*, vol. 23, May/June 2001, pp. 32–33.

it when it gives us longer life with reasonably good quality but it can turn against us with increased suffering at the end. Our interactions with techno-medicine and how they affect us are based on many decisions made over months or years so if we want to die peacefully, we need to give serious thought about the modern way of dying and how we can do it on our own terms.

Planning and Decisionmaking

The antidote for the agony of weeks or months of extended high-tech dying is planning ahead and then participating in medical decisions. Make no mistake, unless you die suddenly or without any medical care, many decisions will be made that will determine the manner in which you die and when. Whether you have another round of chemotherapy, whether you stay in the hospital or go home to die, even something so seemingly simple as whether you have antibiotics for an infection or another blood transfusion—all such decisions have great implications as to how long and how peaceful the dying process will be.

Furthermore, advance planning is necessary because the most important decisions often arise after a patient is no longer mentally able to make decisions. For example, the decision as to whether someone should be treated with an artificial ventilator often comes when that person is unconscious after an operation or a stroke. And the decision whether to go to an intensive care unit or to go home to die often must be made when the patient is heavily drugged or sedated.

The key to peaceful dying is shared decisionmaking, with patient, family and doctors all involved. I'm not suggesting you do it all on your own, just that you participate in making decisions that reflect your values and goals. Remember, "no decision is a decision," because it means someone else will make it for you. Many doctors will be making important decisions that affect you; they tend to "do everything possible" rather than to make decisions based on your choices. If you don't get involved in these decisions, someone else (maybe the doctor on call in the ER) will make them for you. So you have every right to participate and you must participate if you want control over how you die.

But you need the help of your physicians for their expertise in advising you and as your agents who will be carrying out your wishes. You have to be very clear with your physicians and you must have their agreement in advance to help you die your way. Above all, you need the understanding and support of your family because they will be pinch-hitting for you after you cannot make decisions. Without their help in carrying out your wishes, the doctors may not act as you wanted them to do.

Helpful change is in the air—more and more physicians are heeding the pleas of their patients for more peaceful dying. Movements for better pain management and more hospices or "comfort care" units within hospitals are gaining momentum. Some physicians remain resistant to these trends but in general it is becoming easier for patients to assert their wishes for how they die through advance planning and discussions with physicians.

Planning in Advance

Advance Directives What then are the methods and options for planning and joint decisionmaking? Start with written advance directives. A living will is essentially a statement about how you want to be treated when you are dying. This statement tells your doctors what you want done if you are dying and become unconscious or unable to make decisions. For example, would you want to be resuscitated if your heart stopped or would you want to be put on a breathing machine? The living will is a guideline to your goals and choices but you should back it up with a durable power of attorney—a document through which you appoint someone (usually a close relative) to make medical decisions for you if you become unable to do so.

Give these advance directives to your physicians as their guide to your end-of-life treatment. It is important also to discuss them with your family. This is perhaps the easiest way to ease into a discussion of your wishes with close family members so they will know what you want when or if they have to make decisions for you.

Shortening the Dying Process Learn how you can limit suffering at the end of life, if you wish, by avoiding or withdrawing treatments that probably would do no more than extend the final phase of dying. Overall, this is probably the most important and effective way of avoiding prolonged suffering. Most people die in hospitals after their lives have been drawn out far past their natural limits and the point of meaningful existence. But to avoid such futile therapy you really have to plan in advance through discussions with your doctors and family. If a doctor says, "You need this operation," or "another round of chemotherapy," or "a feeding tube," it's almost impossible to "just say no" if you haven't discussed it in advance. Everyone involved must know that you do not want "long-shot" cures that in all likelihood will only add weeks or months to your dying process. Preparing for this takes some time and work but it's well worthwhile.

Hospice and Palliative Care Learn about hospice and the option of "palliative care," which means concentrating on relief of discomfort at end of life. In order to avoid prolonged dying it is often necessary to "let go" and to give up on the notion of a cure. This is not easy and although it is possible to continue to seek a cure and to get effective relief of symptoms, often the search for a cure prevents effective relief of physical suffering. And studies show that when a cure becomes medically unlikely, those who continue trying for a cure do not live as long and have poorer control of physical symptoms than those who concentrate on palliative care. This underlies the concept of hospice programs that provide patients with no "curative" therapy but concentrate on aggressive treatment of symptoms as well as psychological, social and spiritual concerns. For many patients hospice provides the best quality of life during the final weeks or months, with the best chance of peaceful dying.

Aggressive Pain Management Learn about legal and aggressive treatment with morphine or by "terminal sedation," if necessary, to eliminate suffering. Physicians often are reluctant to give morphine or other narcotics even to dying patients. But times are changing. Physicians now have less to fear legally from giving large enough doses of morphine to relieve suffering of dying patients, even if the drug might shorten life slightly, which is actually unlikely. "Addiction" with large doses of narcotics is not an issue in dying patients because the drug is being given for a medical, not a social, need.

However, even today many physicians will not voluntarily give enough morphine to quell all pain. You must plan on asking for more pain relief if you aren't getting enough. This takes some assertiveness but more and more physicians will respond if asked. Also, the family must be ready to jump in and ask for—insist if necessary—better pain relief. If morphine cannot accomplish adequate symptom control, as is rarely the case, it is ethical and legal for a physician to sedate a dying patient to unconsciousness so as to eliminate all suffering. Death ensues for any patient receiving this "terminal sedation" when (also with patient and family request) fluids and nutrition are simultaneously withdrawn.

As with other aspects of end-of-life medical care, you need planning and joint decisionmaking with your family and physicians to achieve these treatments. If your doctor or hospice nurse knows in advance that you want aggressive and maximal pain relief, you will likely get it.

Peaceful Dying

Figure out your goals for peaceful dying and prepare for it. Be in control and ask your family and doctors to understand your goals and help you attain them. To have peaceful dying you should connect with your loved ones. Gather them around you and tell them how much you love them. Settle any unfinished business, interpersonal or otherwise. Seek reconciliation, if appropriate. Ask your loved ones for forgiveness and give the same to them. Seek spiritual peace and readiness in your way. Say good-bye.

Bear in mind that although these nonphysical aspects of peaceful dying are as important as the physical ones, a dying person in physical pain or distress cannot achieve personal or spiritual peace or closure. If you are a loved one, help the dying person reach her goals. Be sure she has enough pain relief to do what she needs to do. If suffering worsens, take charge in asking the medical personnel for better control. Hold her hand and tell her you'll miss her but it's all right if she leaves you. Say good-bye.

Things are changing—you can do it.

Living Wills and Other Advance Directives

Randall K. Hanson

In the following selection, Randall K. Hanson reports that it can be very difficult to execute end-of-life medical decisions without legal documents supporting those decisions. He describes two commonly used legal health directives: living wills and durable power of attorney for health care. A living will allows an individual to express specifically what kind of medical care he or she does or does not want at the end of life, Hanson explains. Durable power of attorney for health care differs from a living will, he notes, in that it gives someone close to the individual the legal ability to make medical decisions for him or her if the individual becomes comatose or is otherwise incapacitated. Both types of advance directives can enable patients to obtain exactly the level of medical intervention they desire in the case of a life-threatening illness or accident, he writes. Hanson is a professor of business law at the University of North Carolina at Wilmington.

An issue that has gained national and international attention involves the medical profession's ability to sustain life almost indefinitely through sophisticated life support technology. Of course, many people are concerned that if they become permanently comatose or terminally ill, that they will be artificially kept alive, causing enormous costs and significant emotional distress for family members. An accident victim who is brain dead but kept alive is tragic, yet not an uncommon incident.

Without written directives in many states, it is very difficult, time consuming, expensive, and emotionally devastating to cease life support procedures, even if the life sustaining efforts are clearly futile. Without directives from the patient, doctors are simply afraid to cease life support techniques for fear of litigation. Adding to the frenzy is a recent highly publicized case where a man refused to pay a nursing home after the nursing home refused to take his wife off a feeding tube. Although there were no formal instructions, the husband as-

Randall K. Hanson, "Living Wills and Other Health-Care Directives," *CPA Journal*, vol. 67, March 1997, pp. 53–54.

serted that his wife wished not to be supported in that manner. In the ensuing litigation, the husband was held liable for the continuing costs since there was no written directive authorizing discontinuation.

Almost every state now recognizes medical advance directives by individuals. Advance directives take many different forms, but they basically tell the attending physician what kind of care the patient would like to have if he or she becomes unable to make medical decisions. Advance directives are becoming more common. Federal law now mandates that hospitals inform patients about advance directives when they enter a hospital. This is indicative of how common these directives have become.

While there are many different types of advance directives, there are two directives that are most commonly used. They are "living wills" and "durable powers of attorney for health care." These directives accomplish distinctly different objectives.

Living Wills

The first concept to be completely clear on is that a living will is not in any way similar to a testamentary will and should not be confused with an ordinary will. A testamentary will, among other things, provides for the disposition of property upon death, provides for the appointment of a personal representative, and potentially names a guardian if the testator has minor children. A testamentary will typically has nothing to do with advance directives, since a will does not become effective until after death has occurred. By contrast, advance directives take effect before death.

A living will is probably the most widely recognized of all advance directives. A living will provides specific instructions which will be followed if a person becomes terminally ill, permanently unconscious, or conscious with irreparable brain damage. The basic purpose of a living will is to retain control over whether a life will be prolonged by life support methods after having been diagnosed as being terminal and incurable. It is basically a declaration of a desire for a natural death.

In a living will, the writer is able to describe the kind of treatment he or she desires to have in certain situations. It is common to expressly allow a doctor to terminate extraordinary means of life support, including the withholding of artificial nutrition or hydration. It is very important to understand that a living will does not allow the selection of someone to make decisions on behalf of the infirm; it is a means to merely express preferences while the person is still able to communicate. The most common format of a living will used in the U.S. provides the ability to choose what kind of care is desired if there is an incurable condition and what kind of care is desired if the declarant is in a persistent vegetative state.

Living wills are recognized in almost every state, but there are different validating requirements in some states. For example, in some states two doctors have to certify that the patient has a terminal condition. Some states will not allow termination of life support if the patient is pregnant. Others provide that if a patient is in a coma, the coma must last for at least seven days before life sustaining treatment can be stopped. Specific state requirements can be obtained from a local hospital. Local hospitals will have on hand information that will accurately reflect the particular requirements in that state.

A living will cannot anticipate every type of medical circumstance that may come up and it only comes into effect when you are terminally ill. Because of these limitations, most people who execute living wills also execute a "durable power of attorney for health care."

Durable Power of Attorney for Health Care

A durable power of attorney for health care is similar to a living will, but it becomes active any time the grantor is unconscious or unable to make medical decisions. This document allows an individual to appoint another to make health-care decisions on their behalf should they become unable to make those decisions. These documents are more flexible than living wills and can cover unexpected situations and events. The person appointed to make medical decisions typically may consent to or refuse medical procedures or medications on the patient's behalf if a physician determines that the patient is unable to make or communicate decisions.

A health-care power of attorney does not authorize the agent to make financial or business decisions for the individual who executed the power of attorney; only health decisions are authorized. Of course, a person who executes a health-care power of attorney must have a person in mind whom he or she can fully trust (usually spouses are named). Most states do not allow health-care providers or nursing home employees to be named as health-care agents.

Most health-care power of attorney documents allow the health-care agent to consent to the withholding or withdrawal of life-sustaining procedures in the event the patient is determined to be terminally ill, comatose, suffering from severe dementia, or in a persistent vegetative state. In addition to life-and-death situations, a health-care agent may make routine medical decisions such as consenting to MRI exams, x-rays, or surgery.

Most states will require two witnesses and certification by a notary public for proper execution. Note that it is very common to execute a living will and a power of attorney. In fact, some states combine both in one document. Both of these directives can be revoked if the grantor changes his or her mind.

Palliative Care at the End of Life

August Gribbin

Doctors and their patients often believe that every means should be undertaken to prevent death for as long as possible, writes August Gribbin, a reporter for the *Washington Times*. However, he explains, this belief can have negative results: Too frequently, terminally ill patients undergo painful medical procedures only to die soon afterwards. According to the author, an alternative to such medically invasive deaths can be found in palliative care, in which doctors and caregivers no longer attempt to save a dying patient's life but instead concentrate on easing the patient's pain and other distressing symptoms to ensure a peaceful death. Doctors can help patients to choose palliative care by becoming more willing to discuss various options for pain management and dying at home, Gribbin asserts.

Dying in America is more frightening and often more terrible than it ought to be, and those who know say it's the fault of doctors. Increasingly, medical and mental-health societies, hospice-care organizations and inpatient advocacy groups are focusing attention on current problems with "end-of-life" care. These engineers of change are attempting to coax physicians and the public to revise their thinking and radically alter the American way of death.

Numerous organizations are addressing the issue. The American Medical Association offers physicians end-of-life-care training (with support from the Robert Wood Johnson Foundation) featuring courses in "communicating bad news," "pain management" and "last hours of living." New York's Open Society Institute funds an educational program called the Project on Death in America, enlisting nurses, social workers, teachers, economists, artists and others in an attempt to "understand and transform the culture and experience of dying and bereavement."

Discussing End-of-Life Care

A recent article in the *Journal of the American Medical Association* indicates why these efforts are being made. According to physician Daniel

August Gribbin, "We Shall Not Fear . . ." *Insight on the News*, vol. 17, February 26, 2001, p. 32.

R. Tobin and psychologist Dale G. Larson, "Patients are dying after prolonged hospitalization or intensive care, often in unrelieved pain." The authors note that patients' preferences for medical care "are not adequately discussed, documented or adhered to," and that referrals to hospice and home care, "which could address these shortcomings, occur late or not at all."

Tobin, a surgeon now practicing palliative care, serves on the staff of the Veterans Administration Hospital in Albany, N.Y. Larson chairs the Department of Counseling Psychology at California's Santa Clara University. The two want end-of-life conversations with patients to become a routine part of health care, and they want such talks to occur earlier rather than later in a patient's terminal illness. The pair are pushing for creation of a new kind of medical specialist trained to lead interdisciplinary teams geared toward the varied needs of dying patients and their families.

In *Peaceful Dying,* his guide to end-of-life care, Tobin provides an illustration of his complaint with the current approach to death in most hospitals. He recalls the last days of a fearful 88-year-old man, "dying of multiple diseases, all very advanced." The man had said he wanted "no more tests" and pleaded to return to the nursing home where he lived. Yet, writes Tobin, "For six days, doctors performed various tests. The gastroenterologist passed tubes up and down both ends to search for tumors. The respiratory specialists were taking blood gases—an extremely painful blood test in which the blood is taken from arteries in the wrists. The primary-care doctors ordered daily blood tests to determine medication changes."

Finally, writes Tobin, the patient's heart gave out, "a full-scale code blue." The staff injected stimulants into the patient's veins and inserted an intravenous catheter into his neck as a doctor pumped his upper body, cracking his ribs. Other members of the emergency team threaded a breathing tube down his windpipe and placed electrical paddles on his chest, causing his body to jerk off the bed with each jolt of power. After 10 minutes, the team determined the man had died during the process.

"Respiratory therapists, five doctors, three nurses and three medical students all looked down at the floor, dejected," continues Tobin. "They had failed in the one thing their training had told them mattered—they had not prevented death."

Achieving a Peaceful Death

The final week of that old man's life might have been different if his wishes had been honored and appropriate arrangements made. He might have gone home. There, he could have been medicated to relieve pain. At his nursing home, skilled practitioners could have relieved or soothed the nausea, fatigue, lack of appetite, shortness of breath, swallowing difficulty and other comparatively small torments that tend to occur during the weeks or months it can take for the body to finally shut down. The patient might have had highly skilled counseling to help him overcome the dread and depression that descend on those who realize their end is near.

There is overwhelming evidence that most people want a serene, pain-free death—witness the legalization of physician-assisted suicide in Oregon and the Gallup organization's findings in a series of national polls from 1997 to 2000. The surveys reveal that between 57 percent and 61 percent of Americans favor physician-assisted suicide under certain conditions.

But not everyone has faith in palliative care. And Tobin's observations defy current mainstream thinking. Indeed, a report by the National Academy of Sciences' Institute of Medicine notes that patients and families continue to demand treatments "that practitioners see as useless, counterproductive or even inhumane."

In the late 19th and early 20th centuries, by contrast, the average person knew much more about death than Americans do today. It was common then for people to breathe their last at home. Children saw grandparents, parents and siblings die.

With subsequent advances in technology, doctors found ways to prolong life and researchers increasingly promised and produced cures never dreamed possible. Death increasingly occurred behind screens in hospitals. Life's ending became for most Americans a mysterious, remote, unseen and dreadful phenomenon.

Barriers to Change

Today, patients don't want to give up hope that they can be cured—or at least escape imminent death. Moreover, the health-insurance system generally pays for the expensive, desperate efforts to prolong life. That tends to bolster the practice of whisking dying patients to the hospital, where they eventually expire while physicians are striving to revive them.

Currently, just 20 percent of those who might opt for palliative end-of-life care do so, although Medicare and most private health insurers cover such care and even encourage its acceptance. After all, palliative care is cheaper, an increasingly important consideration as the aged population expands. Put crassly, it's getting too expensive to keep snatching people from the brink of death.

As Larson and Tobin see it, the chief reason people don't choose palliative care is that most doctors don't give patients with terminal illnesses the facts about their disease. Physicians avoid end-of-life conversations because they essentially view death as an enemy to be defeated. Besides, they fear causing emotional pain and anticipate there will be disagreement with the patient or family members. And many doctors lack understanding of local laws governing what's called "advance directives," the written orders about future medical care that are stated in living wills and healthcare proxies. Additionally, while there is some insurance reimbursement available to physicians as compensation for time spent consulting with terminally ill patients, it is not considered sufficient or sufficiently available.

Psychologist Bruce Ambuel, a professor of family and community medicine at Milwaukee's Medical College of Wisconsin, agrees. "It's hard for doctors to say the 'd'-word—death. It's hard for them to start discussions about it. So although doctors are in a unique position and have the background to make predictions about the outcome of treatment and have a special relationship with patients, they don't discuss the coming death."

Larson and Tobin hope they can change all this and, in the process, make end-of-life care a little more humane. As Tobin puts it, "the living that you do throughout your dying can be, if you let it, some of the most meaningful and joyful living you've ever experienced."

How to Meet Financial Needs During Terminal Illness

Kristin Davis

Dealing with terminal illness frequently means struggling to find money for medical bills, reports Kristin Davis in the following selection. However, she reveals, there is often money to be found in unexpected places. She explains that because most people have not planned ahead for dealing with the expenses of terminal illness, they may overlook certain resources, such as disability benefits, Medicare coverage, and the option of borrowing against or selling life insurance policies to raise cash quickly. In addition, Davis stresses the importance of thoroughly documenting financial assets in order to help surviving family members locate essential papers and to protect heirs from incurring unnecessary expenses. Careful financial planning can reduce some of the stress for those facing terminal illness, the author concludes. Davis is a senior associate editor for *Kiplinger's Personal Finance Magazine.*

Tess and Jack Storke were financially set. They had built a comfortable investment portfolio to see themselves through retirement. They had purchased a second home in Hilton Head, S.C. But their carefully tended nest egg shattered under the weight of the medical bills that accompany a lengthy terminal illness. Jack, now 61, learned in 1994 that the cancer he thought he'd beaten six years earlier had recurred. Their subsequent battle with the disease has been devastating—physically, psychologically and financially. "We had two homes, two cars and money in the bank, and this has wiped us out," says Tess, 55.

Faced with the diagnosis of a terminal illness, your first reaction is shock, followed perhaps by a desire to wind up unfinished business—in particular, "the emotional business of life," says Joan Richardson of the National Hospice Organization. People want to patch up relationships or make contact with distant relatives and friends. They plan the trip they've always wanted to take or a big family reunion.

What families often don't plan for is the drain on their financial

Kristin Davis, "Dealing with Dying: A Terminal Illness Can Obliterate the Best-Laid Financial Plans. But Sometimes There's Help in Unexpected Places," *Kiplinger's Personal Finance Magazine*, vol. 51, April 1997, pp. 90–95.

resources. Their inclination is to put off making a host of financial decisions until the need is critical. Yet you have to squeeze everything you can out of your fringe benefits while you're still on the job. Bills for treatment and medication often overwhelm even those with good health insurance, so you may need to change the mix of your investments or tap your life insurance just to get money to live on. You need to anticipate problems that may arise for your family members. "Financial planning usually takes a back seat, but it should be one of the first things you take care of," says Patricia Drivanos, a New York City financial planner who works with seriously ill clients.

And while you hope for the best, you have to plan for the worst.

A Crying Need for Cash

Jack Storke left his job as a manager with a carpet-installation firm in October 1994, immediately after he was diagnosed with cancer of the head and neck. He had no disability benefits through his employer, and he faced a five-month waiting period for social security disability benefits. At first Tess continued to work as a receptionist at a real estate agency, but she soon quit to take care of Jack rather than pay a registered nurse $150 an hour. "I couldn't make enough money to afford that," she says.

So for five months they had no income, other than a small amount from investments, while the bills for doctor visits, surgery and laboratory tests mounted. Of the social security checks that arrive now, Tess says that "it's income, but it's nothing." (A typical social security disability benefit is about $1,000 a month, according to the Social Security Administration, and can be as much as $1,500 a month.)

To raise cash, the Storkes sold their Hilton Head house and have put their home in Fort Myers, Fla., on the market. They sold their blue-chip stocks and bonds, shifting the money into money-market accounts so it would be easily accessible. That means they've had to settle for 5% returns at a time when the stock market has been soaring.

Making the Most of Work Benefits

Before you tap your own nest egg, make sure you're getting as much as you can out of your benefits at work—a source often overlooked as a resource for the terminally ill. "The worst thing is to find out you have benefits that you walked away from—that you left $250,000 in life insurance on the table," says Drivanos.

• Disability Insurance. Check to see how much income you can expect if you can no longer work and how long you'll have to wait before receiving benefits. If your disability coverage is paid for by your employer, you'll pay taxes on any benefits, which typically amount to 60% to 70% of salary. If you pay the premium, benefits are tax-free. If you have the opportunity to change jobs—as you might in the case of a long-term illness—you may be able to take with you disability insurance you had through your former employer. One of Drivanos's clients pays about $35 a quarter to keep such a policy in force.

To qualify for long-term-disability benefits, you normally must have a doctor certify that you can no longer perform the duties of your present job. (To get social security benefits, you must not be able to do any "substantial work," which generally means work for which you earn more than $500 a month.) Sometimes companies will keep employees with a long-term disability on their rolls as active employees and continue paying their benefits, but in general you can't count on that.

When you qualify for long-term disability, you often become vested automatically in a pension or retirement plan. By law, you can then tap that money without paying the usual penalty for making withdrawals before age 59½. You would still have to pay taxes on the payout, so if possible you'd want to delay taking the funds until the year after you left work, when you'd presumably be in a lower tax bracket.

• Life Insurance. If you have a group life policy at work, you can probably convert it to an individual policy on which you pay the premium. Typically you have 31 days from the time you give notice to your employer to decide to convert—and an employer may neglect to tell you the option is available. The premium may be expensive because you'll probably have to convert your policy from term to cash value; one of Drivanos's clients pays $328 a month to keep $320,000 worth of insurance in force. "But this is one of the few opportunities you may get to have or keep life insurance," Drivanos says.

• Health Insurance. When you leave an employer, you can continue your coverage under the federal Consolidated Omnibus Budget Reconciliation Act of 1985 (COBRA) provision for 18 months; that can be extended to 29 months if you're disabled. Again, you pay the premium.

Short-Term Strategies

As the Storkes discovered so painfully, the double whammy of lost income and increased payments for insurance and medical expenses forces a "flip-flop of traditional financial planning," says Donna Rio, a certified financial planner in Oakland who's also president of a national nonprofit organization called the Affording Care Resource Network. "You have to reevaluate how your money is invested," she says. "Instead of putting money away to grow, you may need to be investing for income and converting some assets to cash."

That means scaling back on risk and tilting your portfolio toward fixed-income assets and investments with shorter maturities and more liquidity. Drivanos says investments should probably be more in line with someone who is 70 or 80 years old—generally 70% to 80% fixed income and 20% to 30% equities.

Ideally, you'll be able to start shifting your investments while you're still earning income. That gives you the chance to stop retirement-plan contributions or other regular investments and instead build a cash reserve that could protect you from having to sell assets—and incurring capital-gains taxes.

You may also have to scale back your style of living. "People in this situation often want to pamper themselves through this, but I encourage them to do that in ways other than spending money," says Susan Bradley, a financial planner in West Palm Beach, Fla.

Managing Medical Costs

The Storkes' health insurance took care of 80% of Jack's medical bills—they had extended coverage through his employer under COBRA—but covering the remaining 20% was a struggle. Tess spent countless hours going back and forth with insurers to make sure bills were paid. And after the bills became overwhelming, she spent even more hours negotiating with doctors to accept less than their 20% co-payment. "I said, 'It's just not there. Can you help us?' And they did," Tess says. When possible they chose doctors who would accept the insurance coverage as full payment.

Now that Jack is a patient at Hope Hospice, in Fort Myers, the medical bills have stopped piling up because he qualifies for medicaid coverage. "We didn't think we'd be eligible because we had too much in assets," says Tess. But because the assets happened to be in her name, they didn't affect Jack's eligibility. (Because he's under 65, Jack would have had to wait for two years after qualifying for social security disability to get medicare coverage for his hospice care.)

Medicare and, in 40 states, medicaid cover 100% of hospice care expenses, including pain medication. Medication for a patient at home can cost as much as $20 to $30 a day, says Samira Beckwith, president of Hope Hospice, and without coverage patients often skip doses because they think they can't afford it, she says.

Beckwith stresses that patients don't have to wait until weeks or even days before the end to seek hospice care. "Hospice is appropriate whenever someone's disease may be terminal," she says. However, to qualify for medicare and medicaid hospice coverage, a patient's life expectancy must be six months or less. Coverage doesn't automatically run out after that time; as long as hospice care is still "medically appropriate," coverage can continue indefinitely. But if you withdraw from hospice care after 210 days, you're ineligible for coverage should you want to return later on.

A Lifesaving Asset

Life insurance is generally thought of as a way of taking care of your heirs. But it can also be a source of cash for you if you need money quickly to cover expenses associated with a terminal illness. It's not uncommon for critically ill people to allow policies to lapse because the premiums are a burden. Because it can be such a valuable asset, however, try not to leave a life insurance plan; you may be able to get help keeping it in force.

Check your policy. It's possible that years ago you signed up for a waiver-of-premium rider, which means the insurance company covers your premium if you're disabled and unable to work. If you can no longer afford the premium on a cash-value policy, see if you can use some of the cash value to cover it. If affordability isn't a problem and you have a "guaranteed insurability" option, you may even be able to buy additional coverage without any medical tests.

It may also be worthwhile to check your credit card statements and auto or home-equity loan documents to see if you've been paying for credit disability or credit life insurance. If you have credit disability, notify the card issuer when you're eligible for benefits, which would cover the minimum payments. If you have credit life insurance on a credit card, make sure your survivors know about it.

In the case of catastrophic medical expenses, a loan or an early payout from a life insurance policy can be a godsend. You could always borrow against a cash-value policy on which you'd been paying a premium for years. Now you have other options as well:

• Accelerated benefits. Both cash-value and term policies—and sometimes even group life insurance—often carry accelerated-death benefits, meaning the company will pay a terminally ill patient as much as 90% of the policy's face value now instead of the full benefit at death. But many insurers don't offer the option when life expectancy is longer than 12 months, and others restrict it to policyholders who signed up for an accelerated-benefits rider when they purchased the policy. Check with your insurer.

• Viatical settlements. Whether you have cash-value or term insurance, it's possible for individuals with a life expectancy of less than two to three years to sell their policy for a percentage of the face value, using what's called a viatical settlement. Payouts typically range from 50% to 75%, depending on life expectancy, premiums and the financial strength of the insurer, says Deborah Rhoades, owner of Viatical Clearing House Inc., in Loveland, Ohio. The buyer keeps up the premium and collects the benefits at the individual's death.

In 1996, Gaetano Toraldo of Old Forge, Pa., needed cash to cover his share of $443,000 in medical bills for a heart-valve transplant—one of four surgeries during the year for chronic cardiac disease. Even with insurance that paid some expenses in full and 90% of others, and after negotiating lower payments with some doctors, Toraldo still faced $10,000 in medical bills. To settle the balance he shopped his $200,000 term policy with several viatical-settlement companies, which offered to pay anywhere from 30% to 60% of the face value.

Then he turned to a viatical-settlement broker, who was able to arrange a policy loan for 70% of the value. With the $140,000, he paid his bills and invested the remainder in his wife's name. "I don't know what's going to happen to me, but the money is there for my wife's future," says Toraldo, 48. At his death, proceeds from the policy will repay the loan.

Payouts from both viatical settlements and accelerated-death benefits are tax-free if your life expectancy is less than two years and if the viatical company is licensed in your state. A viatical loan can be the best route for someone on medicaid, so that a lump-sum payment doesn't disqualify the patient for benefits.

As welcome as the money may be, the viatical process can be unsettling, warn those who have been through it. "People are bidding over your death and arriving at the amount of money you get by how close you are to the end," says "Roy," a San Francisco retailer who has AIDS (and who asked that his name not be disclosed). "It's quite stunning."

Roy received a $220,000 settlement on a $370,000 policy, which he has used to pay for medical expenses, including medication. He takes a combination of AIDS drugs, including protease inhibitors, which have improved both his health and his prognosis. Once told by a doctor that he had two to three years to live, Roy's life now has "no time frame." But the financial strain continues. "I spend about 45% of my monthly income on medical expenses," he says.

The Paper Trail

"Where would my mother have put the green metal file box?" wondered Pamela Davis of Douglasville, Ga., after her mother's death from cancer in July 1996. She knew her mother kept her insurance policies, cemetery-plot deeds and other papers in the box, but she hadn't a clue as to where to find it. While her mother was ill, "we both danced around the issue," says Davis. After two days of frantic searching, she found the box in a closet. Davis's advice: "Sit down as quickly as possible when an illness is diagnosed, and find out where everything is."

Even better is to take an inventory of your financial assets that details what you own, where it's located, what it's worth and whose name it's in. The list should include bank accounts, insurance policies, brokerage and mutual fund accounts, pensions or other benefits at work, retirement accounts, savings bonds, real estate and shares in a privately held business. If you've sold investments, include records showing how much they cost, so your heirs don't overpay taxes. Make a list of any personal property that's valuable, "so a relative doesn't give your Louis XIV armchair to the Salvation Army," suggests Drivanos.

One helpful resource is *The Beneficiary Book,* a binder filled with worksheets for listing everything from financial advisers to feeding instructions for orphaned pets. A good software alternative is *Personal RecordKeeper.*

Whatever you can do to tie up loose ends will ease the transition for family members. But it's also true that taking care of the financial issues associated with dying can improve your own quality of life.

Funeral Options: Planning Ahead

Tim Matson

In the following selection, adapted from his book *Round Trip to Deadsville*, author Tim Matson discusses how people can avoid paying too much for funerals by planning ahead. Matson points out that the funeral industry is a for-profit business; the cost of coffins, memorial services, and cemetery monuments can be exorbitant. Most individuals do not plan their own funeral arrangements before their death, he explains, leaving family members to struggle to make decisions during their time of grief, when they are particularly susceptible to persuasive sales pitches. However, the author asserts, people who plan ahead can help to keep costs under control. Cremation, inexpensive or self-made caskets and urns, and even backyard burials are among the options Matson explores.

Guess what? You're going to die. Not today (with luck), not tomorrow (you hope), but some day. The Grim Reaper waits. Sure, you already knew that, and you try not to think about it. But before you flip the page, let me tell you the problem with death denial (those undertakers who happily profit on death fears can stop reading now). Ignorance may be bliss when it comes to mortality, but it's going to cost you.

A couple of years ago, hitting my mid 50s, I'd heard about enough overpriced funerals and unsatisfactory memorial services to take a stab at saving my relatives some money, and possibly unnecessary grief and confusion, by making my own funeral plan. I was also inspired by the story of a northwoods logger who built his own coffin and slept in it, "To get used to it," he said. Talk about confronting your demons.

I'd already spent plenty of time trying not to think about death. (My favorite ale was a dark brew called Courage.) But how long can you ignore the gray hairs, back aches, and general dilapidation? So I hit the road, dropping in on undertakers and coffin makers, stone carvers and grave diggers, looking for a simple exit strategy. In the process I gained a surprise dividend: emotional peace.

There was a bottom line rationale for my quest. As a tight fisted

Tim Matson, "The Last Thing You Want to Do," *Mother Earth News*, August/September 2001, pp. 60–66.

Vermonter, I don't like the notion of being fleeced by an undertaker when I'm in no position to fight back. Maybe you heard about the unidentified woman who froze to death under a car in Minnesota. In compliance with state law, an undertaker was appointed to handle her funeral arrangements. He planned to collect the usual nominal fee from the state, until it was discovered that the deceased had an impressive estate. The undertaker was able to raise his fee and, according to an attorney in mortuary law, "earn some extra income for a limited amount of work." A nasty preview of the surprisingly common fate many of us will share: Post mortem larceny.

The Development of the Funeral Industry

Strange, how little we're taught about one of life's big events. According to a recent study, 75 percent of hospice patients don't discuss death with their families. Marriage, sex, birth, growing tomatoes—we're up to the neck in life skills information. But death? Leave it to the experts.

There are 23,000 funeral homes in the United States, and they take in $25 billion every year (more than the airline industry and garbage collection). Not bad for a business that hardly existed 150 years ago, when deaths were handled by families, the church, or the local sawbones.

All that began to change with the industrial age. If you couldn't keep people down on the farm, the pursuit of happiness often ended with no one to dispose of the body.

Enter the undertaker (with help from a Civil War doctor who invented an embalming process that made it possible to preserve and transport bodies with one profitable stop at the funeral home). Back then it was called a mortuary, but funeral home had a much nicer ring to it, and the undertaker (make that funeral director) was catching on to a brilliant psychological insight. As Americans lost their intimate contact with death, they were just as happy to forget about the whole damned thing. It wasn't just industrial streamlining that inspired coffin makers to ditch the six-sided "toe pincher." A rectangular shape looked so much less like what it was. Changing the name to casket boosted the antiseptic effect even more.

The Funeral Business Today

The campaign continues today. Over the past decade or so, 10 to 15 percent of the funeral homes in the United States have been bought out by corporate chains whose names have been sanitized of any sepulchral trace; among the biggest is Service Corporation International (SCI). But they've made sure the Mom and Pop funeral parlors they acquired retain their trusted names. However, they have made big changes in mark-ups, often lure unwary customers into lucrative contracts, and occasionally even engage in deceptive deals with church organizations to corral customers. Coffin prices continue to be one of the worst over-charges, even after a Federal Trade Commission (FTC) ruling in 1984 that allowed customers to buy their own coffins. Funeral directors still can charge as much as $1,000 for bring-your-own coffin "handling fees." (Virginia, Louisiana and Oklahoma still won't permit you to buy your own coffin.)

Before the stock market began its current meltdown, the death rush went bust. SCI is on the rocks. Financial analysts chalk it up to overpayment for acquisitions, but customers no doubt are also beginning to shy away from expensive services, especially of the last-minute, unplanned variety.

Avoiding an Expensive Funeral

Consumer advocate Lisa Carlson, head of the Funeral Consumer's Alliance, suggests that an impromptu funeral is likely to cost much more than a planned event. "If you don't do your homework, it's like giving the funeral home a blank check," she warns. She points out that in the age of the internet, it's not difficult to research funeral options and costs on the web. Considering that funeral expenses average $6,000 in the United States, not including cemetery and monument costs (which bring the total up to $8,000, according to the American Association of Retired Persons), there's plenty of opportunity for savings.

So how exactly do you leave this world without being taken for a ride? Begin by asking yourself some basic questions. First, cremation or whole body burial? The funeral industry would prefer to put all of you 6 feet under because that's where the biggest profit lies. To bury a body usually involves treatment in a funeral home, often incurring hefty charges for cosmetology and embalming. Then there's the hearse, burial plot, headstone, and protective vault (to prevent the sod from collapsing on a rotting casket—sorry, in most cemeteries it's the law). Not to mention the coffin, which can cost thousands by itself, most of it in humongous funeral-home mark-ups. Throw in a memorial service, wake, and graveside ceremony, and we're talking real money. Oh, don't forget the flowers.

No wonder so many people are opting for cremation (25 percent now, and the number is rising dramatically). There's a new crematorium in my neighborhood that charges only $550, which includes pickup of the body and personal delivery of the remains. The young owner even throws in a composite granite urn, gratis. When local undertakers heard about this upstart, they tried to put him out of business for operating an unlicensed funeral home. He argued that he was simply operating a crematorium. Big difference, legally. The Vermont attorney general gave him a green light.

After reading about this no-frills rebel, I visited the crematorium (in an old coffin factory), checked out the retort (looks like a maple sap evaporator), and signed up. The average person requires about 40 pounds of gas to be cooked down to a five pound mound of gray ash. The ashes are scooped out of the oven into your choice of container: plain cardboard box, granite urn, or wooden cube, which costs extra.

Discussing Funeral Plans with Family

Alas, the benefits of a quick, low budget cremation may be offset by a regrettable tendency to procrastinate when it comes to dealing with ash disposal. Did the deceased forget to leave instructions? Is the family itself scattered around the countryside, unable to gather for a timely sprinkling ceremony? Showing me around his funeral parlor, one undertaker opened the door into a room full of blue cardboard boxes—unclaimed ashes. If you don't want to wind up a trapped spirit in cosmic limbo, warn your family that you'll come back to haunt them if they ignore your wishes.

In fact, whatever your plans, a family discussion is essential. One bromide of the funeral trade still holds true: funerals are for the living. No sense inflicting unnecessary pain on the survivors.

If you do choose a whole body funeral, you're probably going to need the services of a funeral home. The body is usually transported from the place of death to the funeral establishment, where it is prepared for burial. However, unless the body can be buried within a few days, it may need to be embalmed. If a memorial service is planned with the deceased present, the body is placed in a coffin and transported to the church or synagogue. It's also usually possible to have a memorial service at the funeral home itself. Burial customarily follows the service.

If ever there were a time for planning, this is it. People are often so grief-stricken when a relative dies that rational choices are impossible, and some undertakers cash in on this pain. But remember, plan ahead doesn't mean pay ahead. Many undertakers will try to coax potential clients into signing up for a fixed fee funeral "whenever the time comes."

That may sound like a hedge against inflation, but they can't guarantee how long they'll be in business, or where you'll die. If you want to be sure the money will be there when it's needed, put it in a bank.

Alternatives to Professional Funerals

Fortunately, there are alternatives to expensive professional funerals. Most states allow people to handle funeral details without an undertaker. Options for do-it-yourself funerals include building the coffin, transporting the deceased, and even digging a backyard grave. In many states it's legal to bury a body on your own land, although there is usually some permitting required (including signed death certificate). In circumstances involving contagious diseases like hepatitis B and AIDS, special precautions have to be taken. Check with your state health department and town zoning administration first. The Funeral Consumer's Alliance can help, too. Home burials aren't for everyone, but a resourceful do-it-yourselfer can skip cremation entirely, build a coffin (or simply use a shroud), and dig the grave.

For those who bury their own dead, the motivation usually is less financial than spiritual. Again, the burial plot should be recorded in town documents. There's also a small but growing movement here and in England to "green burials," in specifically designated cemeteries, which dispense with coffins and vaults entirely.

Burial options aren't the only decisions you face. Advances in medical technology have made it possible to recycle various body parts, and many people feel ennobled by the idea of giving someone the gift of life when they die. Clearly, there's no lack of demand, with a national registry of potential recipients that outnumbers donors 3 to 1.

To avoid the potential for ethical abuses, financial rewards are not permitted for organ donation (although the hospital does pay the "harvesting" costs). Donating your body for medical research affords some financial benefits. The medical school usually pays for the cost of cremation, and may offer to bury the remains.

Most people prefer to arrange for the interment themselves. In fact, there's a trend of bringing the deceased home for burial (if he or she isn't there already). With ashes the process is relatively straightforward. The funeral director or crematory operator picks up the body and sends or delivers the ashes. In most states, no permit is needed to scatter ashes on your own property, or the ocean. It's often possible to create a small private cemetery on your land.

Whether you build a coffin, bury a body or help plan a service, it's essential to play a part in funeral preparation to achieve a sense of closure. More than a year after her father's death, a friend still regrets being rushed through memorial preparations by the undertaker. "He handled everything," she said. "I don't feel like I was really involved, it happened so fast."

As for my plans, aside from the choice to be cremated, I'm leaving it up to my family to arrange a memorial service. Surprise me. But forget the cardboard box. I found a fallen maple tree limb and carved it into an urn. It's not big enough to sleep in, but it makes a great cookie jar, while I'm waiting.

Chapter 3

Dealing with Loss and Grief

Contemporary Issues
Companion

Understanding the Grieving Process

Kenneth J.Doka

Kenneth J. Doka is a Lutheran minister and a professor of gerontology at the College of New Rochelle in New York. He is also the editor of *Journeys*, a newsletter about bereavement published by the Hospice Foundation of America. In the following selection, Doka notes that although bereavement is an inevitable part of life, most people are not well informed about the typical process of grieving. Doka stresses that it is important for people to understand the nature of grief in order to help themselves and others deal with loss. The author discusses the different ways in which grief can be experienced. Men, women, and children tend to handle bereavement differently, he writes, and people's cultural backgrounds can also strongly influence the way in which they grieve. In addition, Doka relates, there is no strict timetable for the duration of grief; while the intensity of the pain may lessen with time, grief over the loss of a loved one often lingers for years.

One of the major problems with grief and bereavement is that so little information about the process of grief is widely disseminated. This seems strange for two reasons. First, there is much information that has been learned and studied throughout the last thirty years. And second, and even more basic, loss and transition are natural human processes, existent from the beginning of time. Certainly information about grief and loss should be widely known, an inherent part of folk wisdom.

Yet this does not seem to be the case. One of the most common questions asked by survivors of a death is whether or not their responses are, in fact, normal. And often the response of others seems to invalidate their grief. Others may expect survivors to quickly let go of their grief and get on with their lives. The understanding that grief is a long, uneven process that affects individuals on a variety of levels—physical, emotional, cognitive, spiritual and behavioral—does not seem to be widely known. In fact, a study of clergy indicated that even these frontline professionals underestimated both the nature

Kenneth J. Doka, "A Primer on Loss and Grief," *Living with Grief: At Work, at School, at Worship*, edited by Joyce D. Davidson and Kenneth J. Doka. Washington, DC: Hospice Foundation of America, 1999.

and duration of grief. In a study of television depictions of grief, which both reflect and inform society, researchers found that grief was perceived as a short-term process.

In order, then, to address sensitive ways in which organizations such as workplaces, schools, and churches can address grief and grievers in their midst, it is essential that they understand the basics about grief—what it is, how it is processed, how individuals are affected. That information provides the basis of sensitive response.

What Is Grief?

Grief is a reaction to loss. While we often associate grief with death, any loss can cause grief reactions. For example, we grieve divorces, separations, or other losses of relationships. We may grieve the loss of a job or other work-related changes.

This recognition that loss causes grief can remind us of two critical things: First, during the course of a life-threatening illness, the individual experiencing that illness, as well as family and friends, may experience a variety of losses. In addition to the loss of health, patients, families, and friends may lose dreams and hopes for the future. The individual may experience the loss of work, physical capabilities, or appearance. All of these are likely to generate grief.

Second, any transition, however positive, may also entail loss. For example, a promotion may require changes in relationships with fellow employees, or a move to a new area. Similarly, developmental transitions, such as from childhood to adolescence or middle school to high school, can create a sense of loss. In all these situations, then, grief can be experienced.

Though losses can be due to many factors, this essay will concentrate on losses caused by death, since that reflects the author's experience. But note that much of the discussion and suggestions can be applied to other losses.

Who Grieves? That may seem like a foolish question. Obviously the person affected by the loss grieves. But it is critical to remember that many different people can be affected by a death or other loss. Family members are not the only people who grieve; friends and co-workers may grieve as well. Even people who seem to have a negative connection to the deceased may experience manifestations of grief. For example, co-workers or schoolmates who had an antagonistic relationship may still grieve, perhaps feeling emotions such as guilt, should one party to that relationship die. Negative attachments are still attachments. Even persons who seemingly have little or no relationship may experience reactions at a loss. For example, the death of a younger person or a work-related death might remind everyone of his or her own vulnerability.

How Is Grief Experienced? Grief is experienced many ways—physically, emotionally, cognitively, spiritually, and behaviorally. Each person will experience grief in his or her own distinct way. There may be physical symptoms—pain, headaches, fatigue, lethargy, and others. Emotionally, people may experience a range of feelings that can include sadness, anger, guilt, jealousy, fear, anxiety, longing, and even relief. Cognitively, people may find it difficult to concentrate or focus. They may constantly think about the person who died, recurring memories, or aspects of their illness or death. It is not unusual to experience a sense of the deceased's presence or even to seem to hear, see, smell, or touch that person.

Grief, too, has spiritual effects as people seek to construct some meaning out of the loss. Some individuals may find comfort from their faith, while others experience a sense of spiritual alienation. Grief certainly affects the ways individuals behave. Some may avoid reminders of the loss, while others seek such reminders. Grieving individuals may seem irritable or withdrawn; others may constantly seek out activity as a diversion from pain. The key, though, is to remember that each individual grieves in his or her own way.

Do Men and Women Grieve the Same? From the cradle, men and women are likely to have different experiences. It is not surprising that these different experiences may affect the ways they grieve. Researchers suggest that many men may be *instrumental grievers.* This means that they are likely to experience grief more cognitively and physically than emotionally. Their affect is likely to be tempered. They may seek relief in activity or in thinking and talking about the loss. Many women are *intuitive grievers.* Their grief is likely to be experienced as waves of different feelings. And they are likely to be helped by sharing or ventilating those feelings with others. But again, it is important to emphasize the individuality of grief. Not all men are instrumental grievers, nor all women intuitive grievers. Grieving patterns are *influenced* by gender, not determined by them.

Do Children Grieve? Certainly, but children may grieve in ways different from adults. For example, younger children may not understand death. They may be too young to realize fully what death actually means. Younger children, too, have a "short feeling span," meaning that they only can sustain strong emotions for short periods of time. So grieving children may have emotional outbursts that are followed by seemingly normal activity. But this does not mean children have quickly recovered from the loss. Children may manifest their grief in many of the same ways as adults, but they also may show their grief in different ways. Acting out, sleep disturbances such as nightmares, waking up or bedwetting, regressive behaviors, and changes in school performances—all can be signs of grief.

Different Ways of Grieving

What Affects Grief? The nature and intensity of a person's experience of grief can be affected by many factors: the circumstances of the loss, the type and nature of the attachment, the quality of the relationship, as well as many personal, social, and cultural factors.

First of all, each relationship is different. The loss of a spouse is different from the loss of a friend, child, parent, or sibling—not necessarily easier or harder, just different.

The relationship is not only different in each role, but also in quality. Each relationship is unique and distinctly mourned. Some relationships are more ambivalent than others. That is, they have mixed elements—things one liked about the person, and things one disliked. Often relationships that have very high ambivalence are harder to resolve. Some relationships are more dependent. Some, more intense.

The ways people die are different, and that, too, affects grieving. Often deaths that are very sudden, or follow long, painful illnesses, create problems for resolving grief. Grieving a suicide or homicide is different from grieving a natural death.

Sometimes the circumstances as well as the cause of the death can create special issues for survivors. In one case, Tom had great difficulty in resolving the loss of his parent, in part because the death took place on a day when he was skiing and was unreachable.

Not only are relationships and circumstances different—each person is, too. Each of us has his or her unique personality and individual ways of coping. Some people are better able to cope than others are. And everyone copes with a crisis in different ways. Some will bury themselves in work, seeking diversion; some will want to talk; others will avoid conversation.

A person's background affects grieving. Everyone belongs to varied ethnic and religious groups, each with its own beliefs and rituals about death. Sometimes these rituals, customs, and beliefs will facilitate grieving, other times they may complicate it. For example, perhaps our religious beliefs provide comfort that the person is in heaven or at peace.

Situations may be different as well. It is harder to resolve grief if one is simultaneously dealing with all kinds of other crises in one's life. It is harder to deal with the stress of grief if one's health is poor. It is harder to cope with loss if friends and families are unavailable or not supportive.

The Highs and the Lows

How Is Grief Processed? Grief is rarely processed in predictable patterns—it is a process unique to every individual. It may be helpful to describe grief as a roller coaster, full of ups and downs, highs and lows. Like many roller coasters, the ride tends to be rougher in the beginning, the lows deeper and longer. Gradually, though, over time the highs and lows become less intense.

Often holidays, special days, and the anniversary of the death are the low times. Holidays and special days such as birthdays are heavily invested with memories. It is natural that the pain of loss would be especially keen then. The anniversary of the death, too, is often a low point. Here, even the season and weather remind one of the time of loss. And each date—the anniversary of hospitalization, the date of death, the date of the funeral—may have its own significance.

How Long Does Grief Take? As long as it needs. Again, every loss and every individual is different. The popular misconception of grief is that people get over their losses in a relatively short period of time—perhaps a few months or a year at most. The reality is different. Generally, grief tends, in significant relationships, to be most intense for the first two or so years. After that the roller coaster tends to lessen. While persons still experience lows, perhaps even several years after a loss, they tend to be less intense, come less often, and not last as long. Hopefully, these lows will continue to become less intense with time. But there is no timetable for grief.

Do People Recover from Grief? Recovery perhaps is not the best word. It assumes that grief is an illness that one gets over in time. Rather, grief results from transitions that everyone faces. Once we experience such a significant transition, we are changed by it. One never goes back to the way things were. Life now is different as a result of the loss.

For most people, the pain of grief lessens over time, and they are able to return to levels of functioning similar to before the loss. Some may even experience a sense of growth, new insights, or skills sharpened as they deal with the loss. But they still live with the loss. They may have experiences even years after the loss where the absence of the person is felt keenly. For example, at her wedding, Kathleen sorely missed her grandfather, who had died six years before. She was well aware this was the only wedding of all his grandchildren that he did not live to see.

Other survivors may have more complicated reactions, still experiencing intense reaction to the loss years after. Here, the relationship or the circumstances surrounding the loss often created conditions that made it more difficult to deal with one's grief. Sudden, violent deaths, or losses in conflicted, ambivalent relationships are examples of types of situations or relationships that might complicate grieving.

Grief's Effect on Everyday Life

How Does Grief Affect People at Work? Grief can affect people in many ways. Some people actually use work as a diversion, spending more time and effort there as a way to seek respite from the loss. Others may be easily distracted. They may find it hard to concentrate or focus on work, and their efficiency may suffer. Some may find it difficult to maintain an emotional balance. They may struggle not to cry or seem overtly sad. Still others may be angry or irritable.

When work-related deaths occur, many co-workers may be affected. Not only may they experience grief over the person who died, they also may be influenced by the trauma or death, experiencing a greater degree of anxiety as they work.

How Does Grief Affect Children in School? Children may be affected in many of the same ways. They may feel anxious and insecure. They may act out, showing flashes of anger. They may show regressive behaviors. They may seek attention or seem withdrawn. They may have physical complaints, constantly feeling unwell. Like adults, children may find it difficult to focus or concentrate, becoming easily distracted. Their performance in school may decline. Since many of the manifestations mimic learning disabilities, school counselors and psychologists are well advised to assess possible recent losses as they evaluate students.

Can Grief Affect People at Worship? Certainly, grief has spiritual effects. Some individuals may feel angry. They may feel alienated from God or disappointed in the support they received from their worshipping communities. Others may struggle with their faith as they seek to understand their loss. Still others may experience a renewed appreciation of their faith and their faith community.

Four Ways to Help

What Can People Do To Help? First, listen. Many grieving individuals simply need a safe place to explore their many reactions to a loss. One need not try to make people feel better. Nothing one can say can remove grief. Nor is it helpful to share one's own losses at this point. Simply ask the person how they are and listen as they share their grief and problems.

Second, if you can, share memories of the person who died. Sharing one's own stories and memories can assist persons who are grieving as they struggle to understand the life and the death of the loved one.

Third, offer tangible support. There are many ways one can show one cares, including participation in rituals and contributions to memorials. But there are other ways one can help as well. Asking people how they are dealing with the loss demonstrates support. It is more helpful to be specific in your help—offering, for example, to assist them with work, or helping with childcare or a meal—rather than simply saying, "Call me," or "Can I help?" Bereaved persons may be reluctant to seek help or even be too confused and disoriented to assess what they need.

Finally, watch for danger signs. Self-destructive behaviors such as drinking to excess, suicidal expressions, problematic behaviors, or actions destructive to others are clear signs that the persons may need professional assistance in dealing with the loss. Sensitively assisting individuals in seeking such help shows one's own support and demonstrates caring.

When a Child Dies

Tracy Thompson

In the following article, Tracy Thompson examines the unique kind of grief experienced by parents who suffer the loss of a child. According to bereavement experts, she reports, the grief that follows the death of a child hits harder and lasts longer than any other type. Furthermore, Thompson explains, because modern medical advances have significantly decreased the mortality rate of children in the United States, most people have great difficulty coping with the loss of a child when it does occur. Friends and family members often do not know how to respond to bereaved parents' grief, she notes, leaving them with insufficient support. The death of a child can also weaken a marriage, Thompson observes. However, she concludes, with time and support, parents can overcome their pain and rebuild their lives. Thompson is a frequent contributor to national publications such as *Redbook, Good Housekeeping,* and *Working Mother.*

Had it not been for one small miscalculation, Pat Loder would have recalled nothing special about that March day in 1991. She had spent the morning at her parents' house in suburban Detroit, and it was time to take the kids home for schoolwork and chores, including starting dinner before her husband, Wayne, got home. It was a five-minute drive; she'd made it a hundred times. She remembers that the backseat was full of 5-year-old Stephen's toys and that Stephanie, 8, was telling her about something that had happened at school. She remembers singing silly songs. She remembers three motorcycles coming down the street toward them, off in the distance. She remembers, irrelevantly, that it was the first day of spring.

And then, in the peculiar way the brain registers horrifying events, the memories become a series of black-and-white still photos. She is making the last turn, a left onto their street. And then, inexplicably, one of the faraway motorcycles is right there, so fast it's just a blur, so close her brain can't make sense of how it got there. And then the impact, so jarring it obliterates memory and there is a blank space that seems to last forever but cannot be more than a few seconds.

Tracy Thompson, "When a Child Dies," *Redbook*, vol. 195, October 2000, p. 140.

Then she is sitting on the ground, car and motorcycle one indistinguishable heap of wreckage, and strangers are holding her down while she screams, "My babies! My babies!"

That was all the time it took for the universe to crack open.

A Death Like No Other

For parents, the most horrifying imaginable prospect is the thought of burying a child. Yet it happens. In 1998, the most recent year data is available from the National Center for Health Statistics, roughly 41,500 children under 15 died in the U.S.—2,789 of them in car accidents.

The number sounds astronomical, but in statistical terms it's not: Those traffic-related deaths account for less than 2 percent of the under-15 population. We live in a time and place in which medical advances have made the death of a child a rare occurrence. Unlike the 19th century Victorians, who understood too well what it was like to lose a child—to influenza, say—we do not sentimentalize death. The death of a child makes us profoundly uncomfortable. Too often, that leaves bereaved parents to cope with expressions of sympathy even more stilted than the usual platitudes, or, worse, with silence.

"Parents think that no one else has ever experienced this type of pain," says Diana Cunningham, executive director of The Compassionate Friends, an international network of support groups for families who have lost a child.

"This grief hits harder and lasts longer than any kind we know," says Barbara Rosof, author of *The Worst Loss: How Families Heal from the Death of a Child*. "The image of losing a body part is a pretty apt metaphor. We assume that we will bury our parents, but the idea of burying our kids is just outrageous."

How does a family survive? Painfully, piecemeal, and sometimes in ways that can test the strength of a marriage. Here are some stories of people who did.

First Shock, Then Numbness

Pat Loder was the only survivor of that collision on March 20, 1991. The teenage motorcyclist, who was racing with his friends and plowed at a very high speed into the right side of the car, died at the scene, as did Stephen. Stephanie survived only a few hours more.

Pat was 35 when it happened; today, at 45, her face bears no obvious marks of tragedy. She has used what she learned from her suffering to counsel other bereaved parents, and she and Wayne have had two more children, Christopher and Katie, 8 and 7, beautiful youngsters who bear a startling resemblance to the brother and sister they never knew. Life is good in a way they could have never foreseen, and when she and Wayne look at Christopher and Katie they feel unspeakably lucky.

At first, Patricia thought she would lose her mind. She was cut and bruised in the accident and spent only a night in the hospital, where the nurses gave her drugs to help her weather the first shock. They didn't help. She remembers a strange weeping without tears, until her whole body shook with grief. Then numbness set in.

"If I was told to take a pill, I took a pill. If I was told to sit down, I sat down. You go on autopilot," she says. The sense of unreality lasted for months. "I felt I knew something nobody else knew, that my daughter would be coming home from school," she says. "So I'd make sure I was home. It took quite a while for that to wear off."

In a way, parents do lose their sanity—temporarily. "That period of acute grief, what I call brain shock, will persist for up to a year, and that really makes people feel crazy," Rosof says. The symptoms look like serious clinical depression: sleep disturbance, loss of appetite, difficulty making decisions.

Grief That Never Ends

But grief over a child lasts far longer than the usual depression, which can be over in a few months, maybe a year. "Parents have told me it took them three to five years to reassemble a life they would want to live in," says Rosof. "The good news is it's not a lifetime."

Pat remembers longing for a road map that first year, a set of rules for how to do what she was doing. Some days, the grief was a physical pain, and she could not get out of bed; the thought of having to talk to another person was intolerable She would close the drapes, turn off the lights—and feel guilty for shutting people out. On days she was able to do ordinary errands, she would feel guilty for not grieving properly. She never knew which kind of day it would be; her emotions were like a freight train that operated on no particular schedule, roaring through and knocking her down. She had nightmares. She had unexplained physical ailments. One night Wayne had to take her to the hospital because she was convinced she was having a heart attack. But her heart was fine. The diagnosis for her chest pain: acute grief.

Their friends' reactions ranged from the unexpectedly compassionate to the breathtakingly cruel. One acquaintance told them she knew just how they felt; she was grieving because her cherished dog had died. "Once we were at a retirement party—it was quite a while after the accident, but it was the first time we'd been out—and this person said, 'Hey! How are the kids?' And when we told him he said, 'Oh, okay,' and just walked away. Then there were all the people we hadn't been close to before the accident who showed up at our house afterward with casseroles to make sure we were fed. The people who did the most for us were the ones who would listen to our story over and over."

The Loders wanted to join a support group, but their first effort failed. "We went to a general bereavement group, and we were the only people who had lost children—and two children. We became the focus of the meeting, and we felt like freaks," Pat says. Months later, she and her husband heard about a local chapter of The Compassionate Friends. At first, Pat didn't want to go.

"I would say, 'Oh, take me any place but there.'" But she went anyway, and eight months after the accident another mother started talking about the videotape of her child's death that seemed to run endlessly through her mind. "I thought, Wow, somebody else does this," she recalls. "That's the day I started to listen." And slowly the hard work of healing began.

Pregnancy and Infant Loss

"Would you like to see my baby book?" asks Patty Darby. It is a blue-striped album lying on the kitchen counter of her Towson, MD, home. Inside are pictures of the three boys Patty and her husband, Sean, named Brendan Charles, Kyle Patrick, and Erik Champion. Born at 24½ weeks, they are heartbreakingly tiny—the biggest weighed only one pound, 13 ounces. Born on September 14, 1997, the culmination of five years of fertility treatments, the babies lived only a short time: Erik for 19 hours, Brendan for five days, Kyle for ten.

Pregnancy loss was for many years the stepchild of bereavement programs, says Cathi Lammert, executive director of the national office of Share Pregnancy and Infant Loss Support in St. Charles, MO. "More and more parents are bonding with their baby early in pregnancy."

In part, she says, it's because we know more than ever about the very beginnings of life, thanks to the technologies that have allowed many infertile couples to conceive. The cost: an increasing number of premature babies who don't make it.

At first Patty Darby had been frightened to learn she was carrying triplets, but Sean, an avid golfer, was exuberant. "A foursome!" he said. Then, at 24 weeks, she began to go into labor, and the babies were born by emergency caesarean section. All three made it through the first night, but the next morning doctors told the Darbys that Erik was having serious respiratory problems. Patty was suffering from a uterine infection and running a high fever, and Sean pushed her in a wheelchair down to the neonatal intensive care unit just in time to say good-bye.

The next day, the doctors told Patty that Brendan had a brain hemorrhage. At first, she could not comprehend what they were saying; then she refused to believe Brendan would die and resolved fiercely to care for him no matter what his impairments might be. A devout Catholic, she begged God for a miracle.

"Then one of the neonatal intensive care nurses said to me, 'What's wrong with letting go?'" Patty says. "That really made me think. My father-in-law said, 'Maybe God is telling you what to do through these doctors.' So then we knew we had to let him go, and give him to God." So on the sixth day after giving birth, she and Sean went to the hospital to say good-bye to Brendan, who died in his parents' arms.

After that, she and Sean poured all of their hopes into Kyle. "I could touch his hand in the Isolette," she says. "We read him stories. We made him cassette tapes so that when we weren't with him he could hear our voices. He was our tiger." But on the tenth day, concerned about Kyle's intestines, doctors performed exploratory surgery and discovered that most of his intestinal tract was already dead. Kyle died in the recovery room without ever waking up from the anesthesia.

Patty, 36, retells this extraordinary story calmly, but it catches up with her. "We were blessed with three beautiful little guys," she begins, and then, without warning, tears course down her face. She collects herself and tries to explain: "It was the worst thing that ever happened to me, but also the best. To be able to say, 'We were parents'—to feel that kind of love."

Men and Women Grieve Differently

The Darbys went home to a nursery with three empty cribs and a grief they'd never known, and then the McCaughey septuplets were born. Television was full of the unprecedented event, and Patty could not stop watching, though every image was torture. To Sean, it seemed she was willing herself deeper into grief; he tried to get her to turn off the TV. "We have to move on," he would say. To which she could only reply: "I am not ready."

It's indisputable: Men and women tend to grieve differently, says Rosof. In fact, our culture expects this, which means that men seldom have the opportunity to express their feelings. "The expectation is that they pull up their socks and get back to work," she says.

And yet, whether it has to do with the wiring of the brain or cultural influences or both, men do tend to be better than women at compartmentalizing their pain, Rosof says. Women tend to grieve by reliving an event until, somehow, they can incorporate it into their lives; men grieve by doing. "As stressful as work is, it can be a little bit therapeutic," says Sean.

It is received wisdom that most marriages end in divorce when a child dies. But this is simply not true. One 1990 study did show a higher-than-average divorce rate among couples whose children had been killed in car accidents; but from 1995 to 2000, researchers at the University of Washington have been following 271 parents whose children died some kind of violent death—and, so far, only three couples have experienced marital problems. Shirley Murphy, a professor of nursing who helps run the study, thinks the length of time a couple has been married is important; older marriages may hold up better than newer ones.

Cunningham believes the divorce rate is also low among people who join support groups. "People who seek help are usually the ones whose marriages survive," she says.

For the Darbys, the recipe for survival was "family, faith, and friends," says Sean. But caught in a maelstrom of grief, many people find their religious faith irretrievably altered, or even lost.

"I Just Prayed He Would Die"

"I was really mad at God," says Bonnie Schofield, a 43-year-old mother of two from LaPlata, MD. "We're just getting back on good terms."

Bonnie's son, Nicholas, was born on January 10, 1989, with a rare nerve disorder that causes progressive paralysis. Most babies with this condition die soon after birth, but it took a slower course with Nicholas, a handsome little boy whose sweet disposition made even those first exhausting weeks of motherhood a pleasure. Bonnie and her husband, Scot, didn't know he was sick until he was nearly 2, when it was no longer possible to ignore the fact that he had not learned to walk. Even then, it was months before reality hit, Bonnie says. It was the day she asked a doctor at Johns Hopkins about finding a suitable preschool for Nicholas. "Don't worry about that," he replied gently, "it won't be necessary."

By then, Bonnie was pregnant with Amy, now 9. Their photo album shows a happy little boy surrounded by his family, yet as he grows older he seems progressively listless. In the final pictures, his head lolls helplessly to one side. The last two years were a hellish period of doctors' visits, feeding tubes, and fights with insurance companies. There were long nighttime vigils when Nicholas lost the ability to swallow and Bonnie was terrified he would choke in his sleep on his own saliva.

"Then he got so sick I just prayed he would die," she says. The long wait came to an end one May morning in 1993. Nicholas was running a high fever, which Bonnie suspected was a sign the end was near. She and Scot and Amy, then 2, spent the morning holding him on the living room sofa; he was sleeping, not in obvious pain. Then Scot took Amy to a neighbor's, and Bonnie stepped away to the bathroom. She left Nicholas sleeping peacefully on the sofa. When she came back, he had quietly taken his last breath. He was 4 years, 4 months, and 4 days old. "Even though I had anticipatory grief, it was so very final," Bonnie says now, seven and a half years later. She still spots the number 444 everywhere she goes, on digital clocks, on calculators, on price tags.

Only after her son's death did she realize the toll it had taken on her marriage. Friends since high school, married for eight years when Nicholas died, Bonnie and Scot had drifted apart.

"We had a really hard time," Bonnie says. "You're just mad at everything and everybody, so you take it out on the person who's there." For a time, divorce seemed inevitable. Scot, always reticent, withdrew from the family.

"Finally, I just said, 'I can't live like this. Be with us or not,'" Bonnie says. The ultimatum shocked them both, forced them to start talking. And so, each in his own way, they weathered the storm and came back together.

If Scot's grief was silent, Bonnie's could not be contained. In the first months after her son's death, when Amy was still taking afternoon naps, that break in the day became Bonnie's respite. "I could put her down and cry for an hour."

The Path Toward Healing

Without realizing it, Bonnie had happened onto a mourning ritual—one described by Harriet Sarnoff Schiff, whose 10-year-old son, Robbie, died in 1968 of a heart ailment, in her book *The Bereaved Parent.*

"I am Jewish," Schiff says, "and we have a process called Kaddish. Every day the year after Robbie died, I went to evening services. When you give yourself a grieving time, you give yourself permission to function at other times."

All Bonnie knew was that she was angry at God for allowing her son to suffer and die. Over time, though, she found some measure of acceptance: She now remembers the delight Nicholas brought her, how his illness and death pulled her family together. And had it not been for Nicholas leaving his sister an only child, she would never have had Taylor, the cherub-faced 5-year-old who skids into the kitchen asking for dinner. Bonnie and God, it seems, have established a truce.

This is a hard-won serenity, the opposite of forgetting. Pat and Wayne Loder have told Christopher and Katie about their older brother and sister and how they died, and their names come up frequently. "When they say their prayers at night, they always include their brother and sister in heaven," Pat says.

And Patty and Sean Darby never dismantled the nursery they had decorated, never sold the huge station wagon they had bought in anticipation of having a family. Their stubborn faith paid off. On November 8, 1998, after a relatively short labor, Patty gave birth to a squalling, lusty boy, weighing in at more than nine pounds. His name is Charles Austin Darby, and even before he was joined in the spring of 2000 by a little sister named Julia, he was never in any sense an only child.

Facing the Death of Elderly Parents

Lise Funderburg

The death of a parent is difficult for children at any age, as Lise Funderburg observes in the following selection. Even if an individual reaches middle age before losing a parent, Funderburg writes, the grief and disorientation that follow a parent's death can be profound. According to bereavement experts, she reports, adult children find the loss of a parent to be a life-changing event that often affects how they perceive their place in the world. Moreover, she points out, middle-aged children who have lost both their parents must cope with becoming adult orphans. Just as with other kinds of loss, the bereaved need support and time to adjust to the absence of their parents, the author maintains. Funderburg is a former senior writer for *Time;* her articles appear regularly in several publications, including *Life*, the *New York Times*, the *Nation*, and *O, the Oprah Magazine*.

A few weeks ago, Janet Pincus' father died. She had looked after him for 15 years, ever since her mother passed away. Pincus, now 54, had helped him through heart attacks, a pituitary tumor and gallbladder surgery. Two days before he died, he drifted into consciousness long enough to open his arms to his daughter, rock her in them and make one request. "Just stay with me," he said. That was their last conversation. Since his death, Pincus has tried to keep occupied. In the quiet hours, after a day spent teaching kindergarten and before her husband gets home, she sinks into deep sorrow and longing. "It's a hole, and it doesn't go away," she says. "I never thought about being orphaned until my rabbi said it."

What could be more natural—or inevitable—than death, especially when it comes at the end of a long, full life? How simple a trajectory that is, and yet the death of older parents often blindsides their children, no matter how much time they have had to prepare. "It takes a lot of adults by surprise," says Patty Donovan Duff, a registered nurse at the Bereavement Center of Westchester in Tuckahoe, N.Y. "Our society says, 'Your mother had a very good life; she was 70

Lise Funderburg, "The Last Goodbye," *Time*, vol. 156, November 13, 2000, p. S1.

years old.' Yes, but you've lost your mother."

As baby boomers travel through middle age, many will become parentless within this decade. Already, a quarter of 50-year-olds have lost their mothers, and half have lost their fathers. In a society that continues to shy away from speaking openly about death, it appears this group may not be any better prepared than previous generations for what experts say is a profound, life-changing experience.

When parents are gone, so are the prime archivists of your life. "My father watched my first steps," says psychologist Alexander Levy, author of *The Orphaned Adult: Understanding and Coping with Grief and Change After the Death of Our Parents*. "He paced the floor the first time I took the car out at night." The role parents play is beyond measure—and even reason. "Even people who've murdered a parent go through this debilitating and confusing kind of loss," says Levy, who has observed interviews with young killers.

Philadelphia writer Jane Brooks felt terribly isolated when she lost her father in her mid-40s and, not long after, her mother. "In 16 months I went from being a daughter to being an orphan," says Brooks, now 54. "I was just shattered." Not only had she lost her last guardian of childhood memories, but she also suddenly felt childlike and needy, with no one to go to for help. "I was a single, working mom, and this was not a feeling I was proud of or wanted to share," she remembers. As she interviewed others who had lost parents for her book, *Midlife Orphan: Facing Life's Changes Now That Your Parents Are Gone*, Brooks realized that she was not alone in her conflicted feelings.

Inheritance, for instance, is often steeped in deep ambivalence. "Overnight you inherit what took your parents a lifetime to accumulate," Brooks says. "It's uncomfortable and bittersweet." Her inheritance helped her financially but also came with strings attached—albeit self-imposed. "My mother was extremely frugal," says Brooks, "so sometimes when I spend money, I think she would be horrified."

Settling estates can also stir up family feuds. "The distribution of the parental estate becomes the last statement of who Mom and Dad loved best," says psychologist Levy. "And it can be manifested in the most ridiculous objects: some spatula, perhaps—but it's the one Mom cooked pancakes with every Sunday morning."

Heirlooms, though, can also realign the remaining family. "In some cases, siblings rearrange the hierarchy of the family around the object," says Levy. "Whoever got the dining room set becomes the host for family dinners." Whether dinners or other family rituals will carry on, though, is up to the surviving children. "I think my parents were the mortar between the bricks as far as the family goes," says Paul Kane, 29. Seven years ago, he and his three siblings lost both parents within six months of each other. "After they died, we, as individuals, had to make more effort to get together," he explains. "There wasn't that scaffolding anymore, that structure within the family that had given direction to things for 40, 50 years."

Generally, how siblings relate before the death of their parents is how they will afterward, according to Duane Bowers, interim executive director of the William Wendt Center for Loss and Healing in Washington. The death of parents simply reinforces existing patterns.

That has been the case for Thomas Lynch, who has buried many of his Milford, Mich., neighbors as well as his mother and father. Lynch's 30 years of working at the family-owned Lynch & Sons Funeral Directors is the underpinning of his recent book of essays, *Bodies in Motion and at Rest: On Metaphor and Mortality.* Lynch says his parents' efforts to instill a sense of family loyalty paid off, and the complicated task of settling the estate among nine siblings ("And the IRS was like 3½ brothers more," jokes Lynch) proceeded with mutual trust and respect. His siblings also turned to one another for solace. "There is a sense that we are orphaned, but we are not alone," he says. "My brothers and sisters are the only people in the world who know how it feels to be bereft of these parents."

Amid the sorrow, Lynch says, were unexpected gifts. "We had to make room for the rituals, ceremonies and liturgies that my parents were always responsible for." In the process, he saw his siblings in a fresh, more adult light, and he even rediscovered his parents. "When I look, for instance, at my sister," he says, "I see my mother's wisdom, sensibility, faith and her great tolerance for the imperfections in others."

Such losses often bring new opportunities for reassessing one's life. "Even in mid-life people still defer to their living parents," says the Bereavement Center's Duff. "There's freedom to explore without parental approval how one votes, careers, the expression of sexual preference, marriage, religion," adds Levy. There is also, for many of the grieving children, a heightened sense of mortality and of being fully—and solely—responsible for one's life.

Profound re-evaluations are not unusual, says Ken Doka, a professor of gerontology at the College of New Rochelle in New York and an ordained Lutheran minister. For adults, their older parents' deaths dovetail with a life stage in which the children are already noticing the physical signs of aging. Midlife introspection, Doka says, "is like a Janus mask, with two faces looking opposite ways: 'I've lived this much, and now I have this much more to live.'"

The swirl of emotions that stem from losing both parents is typically negotiated through a tremendous channel of grief, which friends and family—even the adult orphans themselves—sometimes greet with limited tolerance. "This is a quick-fix society," says John DeBerry, bereavement coordinator for the Palliative Care and Home Hospice Program at Chicago's Northwestern Memorial Hospital. "Society says keep busy and you'll feel better."

When Anne Reid's mother died in August, her siblings joined her at the family apple farm in Virginia to help with the funeral arrangements. Afterward, everyone headed straight back to work. "My brother's a college professor, my sister's a schoolteacher, and I had to process the apples," says Reid, 62.

Ira Byock, a palliative-care physician in Missoula, Mont., and author of *Dying Well: The Prospect for Growth at the End of Life,* says intolerance is institutionalized. "What are most leave policies for loss of a parent?" he asks. "Three days? In the workplace, people expect you to grieve for a week and then get on with it." DeBerry says too many people think grief is something to move past. "Grieving comes and goes just like the waves in the ocean," he explains. "Do we ever get over missing someone we love? The goal is not to get over it or recover from it but to reconcile to it."

For the last 18 months of her life, Henry Roy's mother lived with Roy in Philadelphia. They were in and out of hospitals frequently, and he says he put his emotions on hold in order to care for her. When she died in February, he went on autopilot, arranging her funeral and cleaning out her St. Louis, Mo., apartment. "I still feel like I haven't addressed it," says Roy, 47, of her death. It took him six months to clear out the bedroom he'd made for her, and he has yet to go through the belongings that fill his third floor. "I keep saying that I will," he says, "but those are her things; I don't feel like I have the right." Toward the end, when his mother needed to gain weight but had little appetite, fast food was Roy's best chance at getting her to eat. Passing a Burger King now can reduce him to tears.

What would ameliorate grief, Byock suggests, is if, given the chance, we all faced impending deaths more directly. Byock has found that one stunningly simple conversation has helped people tremendously. "To complete relationships," he says, "people have to say these five things: 'Forgive me. I forgive you. Thank you. I love you. And goodbye.'"

Though much of loss is anchored in the past, some people who lose their parents lament a future they will never share. Stuart Chapin's father died when he was 25, his mother five years later. Chapin, now 40, considers what their relationship might have grown into had they lived until he'd passed his 20s, which were so consumed by a desire for independence. "I, like my parents, have sat up with a sick child. I, like my parents, have juggled mortgage payments. You receive when you are young. Now you are in a position to share the experience of being an adult, and there is no one to share it with."

Yet what Chapin regrets more than the end of his relationship to his parents is that his son will never know them as grandparents. "He's now three years old and missing out on the experience of aging," says Chapin. "I remember touching my grandmother's face—the papery skin, the strangeness and yet beauty of that. My parents will only be a story to him," he says. "I will tell the story with as much love and art as I can, but he won't be able to create his own story."

DEALING WITH SUDDEN DEATH

Joanne Lynn and Joan Harrold

In the following excerpt from their book *Handbook for Mortals: Guidance for People Facing Serious Illness*, physicians Joanne Lynn and Joan Harrold discuss the difficulties faced by those who lose loved ones to such causes as sudden illness, homicide, suicide, natural disasters, or accidents. Those who face an unexpected loss often deeply regret that they did not have an opportunity to say goodbye to their loved one, Lynn and Harrold explain. They may also experience a wide range of emotions depending on the nature of the sudden death: For example, if their loved one was murdered, they may be overwhelmed by a desire for revenge, while a loved one's suicide can provoke feelings of guilt and shame. In addition, the authors state, sudden deaths often bring up emotionally demanding issues related to police investigations, autopsies, and organ donation. Lynn is the director of the Center to Improve Care of the Dying in Arlington, Virginia. Harrold is the medical director of the Hospice of Lancaster County in Pennsylvania.

Death that comes suddenly and unexpectedly is what many people believe they would want, but it turns out to be particularly difficult—certainly for families. Neither the dying person nor the family will ordinarily have been prepared, assuming that there would be time to deal with dying someday—"when it is time." Those left behind may regret not having had the chance to say goodbye. Few people will have had any prior opportunity to say farewells or ask forgiveness, or just to tenderly affirm a bond. Survivors may have many concerns: Did the person suffer? Did he or she have any last words? Could he or she have been spiritually prepared? Survivors may have many unanswered questions about those last minutes or hours. Survivors may have many regrets and questions and no obvious way to answer them.

Advice for Survivors

What can you do to survive sudden death? First, be assured that time does help. Just endure for awhile—the overwhelming sense of unreal-

Joanne Lynn and Joan Harrold, *Handbook for Mortals: Guidance for People Facing Serious Illness*. New York: Oxford University Press, 1999.

ity, or numbness, or anger will lessen. So will the wild swings of emotion, if that is what you are feeling. You will gradually begin to make good choices, to move forward in your own life. With sudden death, we are especially likely to keep questioning the events that led to death and to feel little sense of a completed life. Some people have found it helpful to act out what would have been said or done, if only you could have been there, or if only you had had a few minutes to talk. Some survivors dream of the person or see him everywhere for awhile. You might take that occurrence as an opportunity to write down what you would say, even to put it in an envelope and tuck it away.

Sudden death often leaves practical matters in real disarray. There will be children to take care of, or financial matters unsettled, or property to handle. With any luck, there will also be some trustworthy family or friends to help. Share your emotions and check your decisions with someone who is not directly affected by what has happened, if you can. They can tell you if you are making good sense. If you are really on your own, then reach out to some professionals—chaplains, social workers, teachers, professional counselors. Everyone deserves someone to lean on when one is suddenly bereaved. You should also consider continuing with some professional support for awhile. Many people find they need to push themselves into counseling or support groups at first, but later they say that this support turned out to be a lifeline and a great comfort.

Sudden death is not a common way to die now, but it is common enough that it affects almost every family. Sudden death happens in a variety of situations, some of which we discuss.

Causes of Sudden Death

Violence. When a loved one dies from violence, the survivors commonly experience a nearly overwhelming mix of shock, grief, fear, rage, frustration, and helplessness. Not only have you lost the person you love, but you have also lost some of your sense that the world can be safe. You may be fearful that the same thing could happen to you, or to someone else you love. You may feel vulnerable and violated. You may experience frustrated rage at the person who did such a terrible thing, or against God, for allowing such persons to exist. You may be angry at the authorities for having so little control. You may take on some of the guilt yourself, thinking that if you had only been there, come sooner, said something differently, this terrible death would not have happened.

Often the survivors of a person who died violently will have to deal with investigators and the press. This can sometimes add an invasion of privacy to your other burdens, but sometimes talking with the press and investigators actually feels helpful—at least someone cares!

If an arrest is made, you hope that justice will be done. But the frustration can be great if the person responsible is unknown or not caught. A long period of time may pass before the person is brought to trial, and there may or may not be a conviction.

People often have savage, vengeful fantasies about the person who murdered or otherwise caused the death of a loved one. This is an understandable part of the grieving process, but the affected person really must reach out to others to avoid acting on this impulse, or acting on an impulse to "take it out on yourself."

Accidents. An accidental death also leaves the survivor feeling shock, grief, and a sense of supreme unfairness. The world may seem much more unpredictable and unsafe. At times, having a clearly identifiable reason for the accident means that some person or agency must bear the blame and guilt of having been careless or thoughtless. You might pursue legal action to ensure that this kind of accident never happens again, or that the person responsible is punished. This can be a comfort that others will not be hurt, or a source of bitterness that a loved one's death is what it took to make a change.

Of course, sometimes the person most to blame is also the person who most loved the one now dead. If you survive in such a situation, you will need to hear many times that others do not hold you responsible, and that you can forgive yourself. You will need to feel the special love of a family or community to begin to make sense of such an event. Do take every opportunity to reach out to others, and make yourself go for professional counseling in the months following the event.

Natural Disasters. Any sudden death makes one feel uncertainty and fear. The world abruptly feels quite unsafe. A natural disaster forces you to feel how small and unprotected we are against the forces of nature. It is no wonder that you may think God picked your own little corner of the world to attack. Added to the loss of a loved one, survivors may have to endure the loss of cherished belongings—even the loss of a whole way of life. You might have to postpone grieving for the dead because of the immediate needs of finding shelter, locating other family members, or dealing with insurance companies.

Survivors of a natural disaster often find comfort in the fellowship of other survivors and in the companionship of community rebuilding. This sense of reconstruction can be the forerunner of healing and the repair of families shattered by the loss of loved ones.

Dealing with Suicide

Suicide. Death from suicide often hurts terribly because the person who has died has so completely rejected his or her family and friends. If the suicide comes after serious physical or mental illness, though, you may feel both grief and a sense of relief that a long period of suffering has ended. You may feel really angry toward the person who has died, particularly if she either gave no warning at all or had actually engaged a lot of your time and energy trying to help. Guilt is common; you wonder if there was something more someone could have done.

If the suicide is unexpected, you may wonder if you and others missed a signal or a silent plea for help. You may spend a great deal of time trying to understand what life must have been like, no longer wanting to live. Why didn't he love me enough to stay? Why wasn't my love enough for her to want to stay?

You may feel ashamed, feeling that this reflects shortcomings in you and your family. Some people will hide the actual cause of death from others who may not understand or might judge harshly.

Families that have been affected by suicide should usually avail themselves of help from a mental health professional in the ensuing year. Family members benefit from a nonjudgmental but insightful outsider who can help sort out the conflicts and watch for signs that the survivors might be developing serious problems in coping.

Multiple Deaths. When you have to endure the pain of the loss of more than one family member or friend, such as might happen in an accident or a natural disaster, grieving becomes more confusing and complicated. Many people find it so painful that life seems especially hollow. Sometimes a survivor wishes he or she could just die also. It may seem as if the dead persons are in a better place, and that it is the survivors who feel left behind. Sometimes you don't know which person to grieve for first, or most, or you feel guilty over missing one person more than another. The losses are so much that you cannot believe that something this terrible could happen and leave you still living. You will often have lost the family system that was there, and you will often feel disoriented without that familiar structure.

Again, you need an understanding of what happened, friends and family to lean on to hear your grief and to give practical help, and a professional counselor. In these circumstances, you must be gentle with yourself and expect that merely enduring is enough for awhile.

During Chronic Illness or Recuperation. When you believe someone you love still has time to live, despite a severe illness, their sudden death will feel startling. When your loved one was stable just a few days ago, you can feel cheated and angry that you were robbed of the time you thought you would have together. Having already endured the anxiety of the illness and begun to face the eventuality of death, it often seems unfair not to get more warning. It may sound odd, but families of most people who die after years of serious heart failure, and about a quarter of people who die of cancer, say that the person died "suddenly." This is not something that even doctors recognize, so usually no one told you that your loved one might well die suddenly. Nevertheless, the death is not a complete surprise, and your mind will usually have made some adjustments to the eventuality.

You can take some comfort in knowing that the person is spared the worst that the disease can yield. At times, you may be frankly relieved that death came suddenly, particularly when your loved one has been ill for some time and faced a long period of suffering. But this relief can cause guilt, too. Survivors are often afraid that the feeling of relief will seem like happiness that death occurred. It is valuable to realize that our feelings of relief are motivated by love and concern for someone we love. Relief that suffering was avoided does not make the grief less real or wrenching.

Sudden Infant Death Syndrome. The death of a child is a heartrending loss. People might expect their parents or grandparents to die, but no one expects children to die before their parents. When an infant appears healthy, as in the case of SIDS (Sudden Infant Death Syndrome), parents are especially stricken. You fear you did something wrong, or didn't do something that should have been done.

Sometimes the appearance of the baby who has died from SIDS can be confusing. Although some infants look as though they are just sleeping, if some time has passed before it is realized that the baby is dead, blood can pool in the baby's face. To inexperienced eyes, this can look like bruising. It is not surprising, although it is very hurtful, that emergency workers, the police, or even family may think that someone deliberately hurt the baby. Such confusion can lead to terrible misunderstandings or accusations. Sometimes parents believe a sibling, or one's spouse, may have struck the baby.

Even after SIDS is diagnosed, it is natural for parents or other caregivers to wonder if something was done wrong which could have prevented the death. Parents report being plagued with the thought that they should have tried to wake the baby from his nap sooner, or that they should not have slept in on that morning, or that she should have been put down on her tummy, or on her back. We so desperately need to find a reason, a way to comprehend the incomprehensible.

No amount of foresight or care can prevent SIDS. Although SIDS happens most often at night, babies have been known to die in car seats and even while being held. You could not have prevented what happened. Nothing that you or anyone else did, or didn't do, caused your baby's death. Networks of parents who have experienced this loss do seem to help one another a great deal. If you have to endure this loss, be especially gentle with yourself and your spouse. Because this death is unexplainable, it will often cause real strains between a couple. Professional help is probably worth pursuing.

Special Issues

Police, Autopsy, and Organ Donation. In addition to the unexpected loss, sudden death often brings with it the need to deal with investigating authorities. Emergency workers, such as the fire department and the police, may have to ask questions. While these people are only doing their jobs, it can be difficult for the family of a loved one who has died to understand, and hard to cooperate. Sometimes the authorities will keep you away from the body of your loved one, either because an investigation is ongoing, or because of the condition of the body. You will eventually get to be left alone and will be able to see the body, but no one may think to tell you so. Many police and emergency services are beginning to consider how to serve survivors better. You might ask if there is a chaplain or someone like that who could accompany you, or you might insist on having a friend or family member along.

Sometimes there is confusion about what exactly did happen. There can be misunderstandings and miscommunications. At times like these, it is worthwhile to keep in mind that some questions may not be able to be answered accurately right away. It is hard to be patient, but it is better to have to wait for a correct answer than get a hurried answer which turns out to be false.

In all cases of sudden death, the medical examiner will be notified and will decide whether an autopsy is required. An autopsy is a special examination of the body that often can determine a great deal about exactly what happened. The body is left looking normal and appropriate for family members to see. Nevertheless, people feel queasy about autopsy. At least in sudden deaths (except perhaps when there is serious chronic illness as the cause), the decision about autopsy is mostly out of your hands. If you have a strong religious objection, you should voice it, but the medical examiner is generally authorized to ignore your claim if there is any suspicion of foul play.

Sometimes members of the media want to ask questions. It is important to remember that you have a right to refuse to talk to reporters and to request to be left alone. If necessary, enlist the help of the authorities or friends or family members to ensure your privacy.

Among the people waiting to talk to the bereaved family may be medical personnel who want a decision about organ donation. In the case of sudden death, particularly if the death itself takes place in the hospital setting, any undamaged organs of the patient are ideally suited for helping someone else. It can be very difficult in the midst of shock and loss to hear about someone else's needs. If your family member wrote out his or her wishes on a driver's license or an organ donor card, then you can be fairly comfortable in following those choices. If not, you need to know that any decision you make will be supported by the care team.

The Impact of Sudden Death

Many Americans believe that a sudden death is what they would want—preferably a sudden death in advanced old age. However, it is clear that a truly unexpected death is very hard on families and often deprives the dead person of the opportunity to complete a life. Nevertheless, about one-tenth of all dying is truly unexpected, and our community must learn to help support those who are personally touched by sudden tragedy.

The Importance of Retrieving the Dead

Robert Sapolsky

In the following article, Robert Sapolsky examines the various reasons why humans find it so important to retrieve the bodies of the dead. Survivors will go to great lengths to recover the bodies of the deceased, Sapolsky observes; for example, he reports that in the wake of the destruction of the World Trade Center on September 11, 2001, tremendous efforts were undertaken to find as many bodies or body parts as possible. He explains that the bereaved feel an overwhelming need to have something concrete to which to say goodbye, even if it is only part of their loved one's body. Retrieval of a body also puts to rest any lingering questions of whether the person may still be alive, the author relates, and in some cases may be crucial to determining how the person died and whether foul play was involved. Sapolsky is a professor of biology and neurology at Stanford University in Palo Alto, California.

In 2001 I got a phone call that I'd been waiting for since 1973. That year I was 16 years old and a student at an alternative high school in New York City. My schoolmates and I were wanna-be hippies, jealous of our older siblings who'd gotten to live the 1960s. That summer there was a rock festival upstate at Watkins Glen that turned out to be one of the biggest ever. Among the 600,000 who made the pilgrimage were two of our friends: Bonnie Bickwit, with her peasant blouse and bandanna, and Mitchell Weiser, with his ponytail. They met up at the summer camp just outside the city where Bonnie was working and hitched to the rock festival. We never saw them again.

Everything we knew about Bonnie and Mitch convinced us they hadn't run away. Something had happened to them. Throughout that fall, we talked to grizzled rural sheriffs and reporters. We spent our weekends posting pictures of Bonnie and Mitch in the East Village in Manhattan, near the buildings of cults that were rumored to kidnap kids. We had nightmares about rape and torture and murder. The loss of these friends was a galvanizing event in my adolescence. Ultimately, it turned out to be the longest unsolved teen disappearance in the nation's history.

A Mystery Is Solved

Then suddenly the long search ended. Mitch and Bonnie's classmates had gathered for a 25th reunion. A ceremony held in their memory got some news coverage. The right person saw a report on a missing persons show and called the police.

The man told police that a teenage couple he had encountered leaving Watkins Glen had drowned. The couple fit the description of Bonnie and Mitch, and the details of the man's story rang true. The news quickly spread by phone and e-mail among people who now barely remember each other. Amid the muted excitement, we all kept coming back to the same issue: If this man's story is true, the bodies of Bonnie and Mitch should have been found. Show us the bodies, we thought, and the mystery of their disappearance will be resolved once and for all.

Recovering Bodies

The desire for tangible proof of the death of someone we know or love is a natural human impulse. But often that desire extends well beyond a purely rational need for certainty. In circumstances where there is not the remotest chance that someone is still alive, we still expend great energy and often put other lives on the line in order to retrieve the dead. Consider, for example, the extreme risks taken by an international team of divers in the fall of 2001 as they worked around the clock for more than two weeks in choppy waters off the coast of Norway to recover corpses from the sunken Russian submarine *Kursk*. In the wake of the terrorist attacks on September 11, 2001, the intense emotional longing that is often associated with efforts to recover remains was especially pronounced. As the days and weeks passed following the collapse of the World Trade Center towers, the United States was brought to an awed silence by the nearest thing we've had in generations to a holy national rite: the search for the dead at Ground Zero.

The quest to get the body back is a drama played out in an endless variety of settings. In Chile, for instance, where civilians of the wrong opinion vanished during the murderous reign of Augusto Pinochet decades ago, the now-elderly mothers of the disappeared still gather to demand: "Give us even a single bone of our children." Sometimes the demand for remains crosses national or cultural boundaries and is passed down from generation to generation. Recently Spanish authorities returned the body of a chief to his native Botswana more than a century after it was stolen from its fresh grave by looters and carted off for display in a museum. An even longer-standing dispute was resolved in 1993 when the Japanese made reparations for a 1597 invasion of Korea by returning some grisly spoils of war: 20,000 human noses.

Cultural Attitudes Toward the Dead

It is tempting to assume that such a widespread obsession with retrieving bodily remains is rooted in a deep-seated human need to ritualistically put the dead to rest in a respectful manner: In the words of an old blues song, "See that my grave's kept clean." But, in fact, death rituals vary dramatically from culture to culture. While most societies traditionally bury or cremate their dead, others such as the Masai in East Africa discard corpses for scavengers. And even among cultures that bury their dead, the sense of a grave as hallowed ground is not necessarily shared. As late as the 19th century in northern Europe, burial was akin to leasing an apartment: Graves were intermittently dug up and the remains discarded to make room for the next tenants. While the Western model of death involves grief and whispered respect, the Nyakyusa in Malawi have ornate funerary rituals of mocking the deceased.

Cultures even differ as to when they decide someone is good and dead. And sometimes individuals who we would consider robustly alive are treated as deceased. In traditional Haitian society, if a person does something deeply taboo, a shaman turns the miscreant into a slavelike zombie; thereafter, the community believes he inhabits the world of the dead. Conversely, some societies continue hearty, active interchanges with people who are no longer alive. In traditional Chinese society in Singapore, younger siblings have to wait their turn to get married, so sometimes an older sibling who dies unwed is betrothed in a "ghost marriage" to someone appropriate and deceased. Even in our own culture and others that are preoccupied with retrieving the dead, with sufficient passage of time (and with the demise of the immediate kin of the deceased) the respectful act becomes just the opposite. Although we consider it a moral imperative to try to recover corpses from the *Kursk*, doing the same to any skeletal remains on the *Titanic* would be seen as inappropriately disturbing the dead.

Reasons for Retrieving the Body

So why do we go to extraordinary lengths to get the body back?

The most obvious reason is to make sure the person is really dead. Until the invention of the modern stethoscope about 185 years ago, determining if someone was dead or just in a coma was often difficult. The fact that some people were buried alive gave way to laws in the 17th century mandating a waiting period before burial; aristocrats stipulated in their wills that bodily insults intended to wake the not-dead, such as cutting off toes, were to be inflicted on their corpses. By the 19th century, inventors offered coffins with escape hatches. In

German deadhouses, which served as way stations before burial, the fingers of corpses were attached to alarm bells. Just in case.

Many nonhuman primates also take time before literally letting go of their dead. This is something that I have observed in my own studies of baboons. An infant dies, and rather than discarding the body, the mother carries it around for days afterward. Sociobiologists argue that there is an evolutionary reason for such behavior: Females who have the occasional offspring revive from a coma pass on more copies of their genes.

With humans, the desire to get the body back is intertwined with the irrational energy that we put into denial. Beginning with our first toddler encounter with a dead robin in the backyard and our parents' uncomfortable "It's only sleeping," the Western model of death is one of euphemism and denial. As first demonstrated in the landmark work of Elisabeth Kübler-Ross, people in our society tend to react to death or the news of terminal illness with a stereotyped sequence of stages: denial, typically followed by anger, bargaining, depression, and if one is lucky, acceptance. In the context of the euphemistic model of death—Grandpa simply goes to the hospital and does not come back—the process of mourning is viewed as hitting bottom in order to move past the denial stage. Thus the tendency of so many of us to consider it a bracing necessity to take the bull of denial by the horns and ask that the coffin be opened, so that we can look upon our loved one's face. For that, we need the body.

Sometimes we want the body back in order to learn how the person died. This can be a vast source of solace: "It was a painless death; he never knew what was happening." The quest for how involves the ghastly world of forensics, where sequence is everything: "She was already dead by the time X was done." And at times the solace comes from learning something about the deceased by the nature of his death: the heroic act, the sacrifice that affirms a group's values. In his story "A River Runs Through It," Norman MacLean wrote of the youthful murder of his hell-raising brother. He had been beaten to death by thugs unknown, and the autopsy revealed that the small bones in his hands were broken. And thus, "like many Scottish ministers before him, [MacLean's father] had to derive what comfort he could from the faith that his son had died fighting." Similarly, many people were relieved to discover that passengers on the hijacked plane that crashed in Pennsylvania on September 11 had apparently put up a valiant struggle.

Spiritual Dimensions of the Body

The desire to get the body back is also sometimes associated with what we believe to be the spiritual well-being of the dead. The Tlingit of Alaska, for example, believe that a body must be recovered for reincarnation to occur. Among the Nuba of Sudan, men are circumcised only after death, a prerequisite for an afterlife. A top-of-the-line Church of England funeral requires a body that can be blessed and put to eternal rest. Some cultures need not only the body but all of the body. Orthodox Jews save teeth, amputated limbs, and excised appendixes for eventual burial; that is why some Israelis will comb the site of a terrorist bombing for scatterings of shredded flesh.

Another major reason for wanting the body back is for the well-being, spiritual or otherwise, of those in control of the body. In *Grave Matters,* a surprisingly entertaining book on cross-cultural aspects of death, the anthropologist Nigel Barley writes, "The dead do not own their corpses." Funerary ritual, with the body as its centerpiece, is an unmatched opportunity to share, affirm, inculcate, and revitalize group values. A well-scripted funeral for a political martyr can galvanize potential crusaders into a self-sacrificing, homicidal frenzy. On the other hand, Barley argues, few settings match a state funeral as an opportunity for a government to signal power and solidarity. Consider the seemingly odd act of the atheist Soviet Union of the 1920s in preserving the body of Lenin in perpetuity like some Slavic saint. The message to the Russian peasantry: "We have crushed and replaced the church."

Glorifying the Dead

The group value of a funeral holds even when it is not for the mighty. Consider how we eulogize the dead. The overwhelming pressure is to glorify, exalt, and exaggerate the good acts of the person. This can sometimes involve downright invention if the person was a scoundrel or if the eulogist is a hired gun who didn't actually know the deceased. In our society the good acts are drawn from a list heavily featuring fidelity, devotion to young children and aged parents, religiosity, a robust work ethic, and a fondness for barbecuing. On a certain level, the concrete rituals of a funeral are lessons for the next generation. The values eulogized represent a remarkably effective vehicle of conformity, producing that superego of a whisper in the ears of so many of us: "How do I want to be remembered?"

Thus the pressure at a funeral to make the deceased seem like a saint. And when the funeral is for someone whom that society really does consider a saint, watch out. When Khomeini died in Iran, frenzied crowds of mourners were so eager to touch their beloved ayatollah [Islamic religious leader] that they tipped over his coffin and shredded his burial shroud. Nigel Barley tells the story of the death in 1231 of Elisabeth of Thuringia, someone so clearly bound for sainthood that a crowd quickly dismembered her body for holy relics. Even more bizarre is the story of the 11th-century St. Romuald, who in his old age made the mistake of noting plans to move from his Umbrian town; the locals, worried that some other burg would wind up with the holy relics of his body, plotted his murder.

Protecting and Honoring the Dead

The body can be a vehicle for resolving cultural conflicts. After a small Japanese fishing vessel was accidentally sunk in 2001 by a Navy submarine, the U.S. government mounted a multimillion-dollar effort to recover the dead. A professor of religion advised officials on the culturally sensitive wording to be used in military communiqués about the operation. Corpses were raised to the surface after dusk and, in accordance with Buddhist tradition, placed in body bags feet first.

By contrast, sometimes a body can be a vehicle for one society to express values that are hostile to another society. There is a Maori tale of a man, grievously injured in battle, who begs his comrades to quickly cut off his head and retreat with it so that it won't be appropriated, shrunken, and displayed as a trophy by the enemy. As a corollary, recall the visceral power of the image of American dead being dragged through the streets by crowds of Somalis. When Zaire's kleptocratic ruler Sese Seko Mobutu was in the final days of his dictatorship, he is believed to have spent his time exhuming the bones of his ancestors so that they would not be desecrated by rebels. Likewise, even though there was no immediate threat of hostility when the United States gave up the Panama Canal, bodies were disinterred from the American cemetery and shipped home along with the microwave ovens and VCRs.

No Closure Without a Body

In the case of Bonnie and Mitch, my schoolmates and I realized years ago that they were never coming home. But because we never got the bodies back, there will always be a measure of uncertainty about what happened to them and about the man who finally made that phone call to the police. Allyn Smith was 24 at the time of the Watkins Glen rock festival. On the way home he hitched a ride in a Volkswagen bus. There was a scrawny young couple riding in the back, also hitching from the festival. Smith and the driver smoked a joint. It was a hot day and there was a river nearby. They stopped, planning to cool off in the water. As Smith crouched to take off his shoes, wondering at the wisdom of going in the rough water, he heard a shout. He turned to see that the girl was in the river. The boy—her companion—leaped in to try to save her. Then they were both swept away, down the rapids, still very much alive.

That is the story Smith told the police. No names were exchanged in the van, but he overheard the two talking about a summer camp where the girl had worked and recalled identifying details about her clothes. It would appear that the couple had been Bonnie and Mitch. Smith is now cooperating with the police, trying to identify the stretch of river where he says they disappeared. "I felt he was credible," says Roy Streever, the investigating detective with the New York State police. Nonetheless, something didn't happen that day. Smith, an athletic Navy vet, didn't try to rescue Bonnie and Mitch. Nor did the driver of the bus. Eventually they drove off. At the next exit, Smith got out and headed in another direction. The driver said he'd make an anonymous phone call to the police from a gas station and report that the two kids had been swept down the river. Police have no record that a call was made.

The parents of Bonnie and Mitch had to cope not only with the loss of their children but also with a burden of horrible uncertainty. One father and one stepfather went to their graves never knowing what had happened. The rest of us finally got the answer to the mystery that plagued us for decades.

Once we were kids who believed enough in our immortality that we would hitch rides with strangers. Now we flaunt the same irrationality by cheating on our low-cholesterol diets. Once we had not yet learned that life brings tragedies beyond control. Now we wonder how we can spare our own children from that knowledge. Once we lost two friends and could only imagine florid, violent sins of commission. Now, instead, we have a doughy, middle-aged lesson about the toxic consequences of quiet sins of omission and indifference.

Sometimes, when you get the body back, or at least find out the whole story, you learn something critical about the nature of the living and of those who knew all along what happened.

Ways to Support a Bereaved Friend

Victor M. Parachin

One of the times in life when people most need the support of their friends is after the death of a loved one, explains Victor M. Parachin, an ordained minister and a freelance writer based in Claremont, California. In the following selection, he suggests eight ways in which friends can help the bereaved in their time of grief. It can take a long time for the bereaved to work through their emotions, the author stresses, and friends need to lend their support throughout the entire grieving period by calling and visiting often. He notes that friends should offer their help through specific and concrete suggestions rather than a vague statement such as "Let me know if I can do anything." In addition, Parachin points out, the grieving often simply need someone to listen to them without minimizing their loss. Appropriate support from friends, he concludes, is vital to the recovery process.

"For months after losing Milton, after more than 40 years of an intensely happy marriage, I was in a state of despair regardless of my being financially secure with a satisfying career. All my lecturing, writing and traveling seemed meaningless without my husband to share it. I was overcome by agonizing loneliness."

The woman describing these feelings is best-selling author Joyce Brothers. Although she is a psychologist who is knowledgeable about the grieving process, her academic and professional expertise did not make her personal loss easier to bear. And she is not alone. Currently, there are 2.1 million widowers in the United States. Of those, more than 550,000 were left with young children to raise. The bereaved need the gentle support of their friends and family whether they've lost a spouse, parent, grandparent, child or friend. Here are eight ways to help someone through a time of grief.

How to Help

1. An effective way to deliver comfort is through a short written note. Unlike a phone call, a letter can be saved to be read again. When writ-

Victor M. Parachin, "When a Friend Needs You," *American Fitness*, vol. 17, January 1999, p. 58.

ing, share a personal memory of the deceased. Etiquette specialist Letitia Baldridge cites the following as an excellent example of a helpful condolence letter:

"I remember the first time I met her in college. I was a freshman and she was a 'sophisticated' sophomore. She found me in my room battling a bad case of homesickness. In fifteen minutes she had chased the blues away by giving me a tour and introducing me to 20 of her friends. She remained that way throughout her life, helping people and offering kindness. She was always ready, strong, creative and compassionate. Your loss is crushing to me, too. I will miss her dearly."

2. Call and visit often. In the weeks and months following a funeral, the bereaved experience a slight letdown as friends and family return to their normal routines. At this time, loneliness can feel overwhelming. A call or visit from a friend can be a powerful antidote to those deep feelings of loneliness. In order to make your visits and calls truly effective, authors Candy Lightner and Nancy Hathaway offer these insights in their book, *Giving Sorrow Words:*

"You might ask, 'Is there something I can do?' But be prepared for the answer to be, 'There's nothing anyone can do.' Then ask, 'What would you like me to do?' Offer specific suggestions, such as, 'Do you want to talk?' 'Would you like some company?' 'Do you need to get out of the house?' 'Would you like to take a walk or drive?' 'Would you like to see a movie?' Sometimes your questions can help clarify their needs."

Patience and Understanding

3. Recognize that recovery takes time. Be patient with the grieving and encourage your friend to be patient. There is no quick fix for the pain of grief. In the early months of grief, it's difficult to do even minimal chores. Generally, it takes the bereaved nearly three years before they begin to experience more good days than bad.

Consider the experience of writer Lois Duncan. Her 18-year-old daughter, Kaitlyn, was the victim of a random shooting. "For months after Kait's death, I'd lie on my bed for hours, unable to focus my mind," Duncan writes. "Just the shopping and housework took all the energy I could muster. Well-meaning friends asked, 'When are you going back to work?' They didn't understand I was too drained to be productive and, when the time was right to return, I'd know it."

4. Listen with your heart. "The reason we have two ears and only one mouth is that we may listen the more and talk the less," noted Greek philosopher Zeno of Citium. The pain of grief is eased when mourners have a nonjudgmental friend who will listen from the heart. Make it as easy as possible for your friend to speak whatever is on his or her mind and heart.

David, a young widower with two school-aged children, advises, "Be supportive and allow us to speak openly about our feelings. Resist the urge to speak about a loss you may have experienced. This was our loss and we need to experience it in our own way. Be there to listen—it is the most precious gift you can offer. The people I found most helpful made no attempt to distract me from my grief. They encouraged me to share my feelings over and over. Each time I told my story, a layer of pain was peeled away and the intensity of grief was eased."

Acceptance and Validation

5. Encourage grievers to accept all of their feelings. The shocking news of a death unleashes a myriad of confusing and conflicting emotions, including anger, depression, guilt, regret, rage, frustration, fear, anxiety, helplessness, loneliness and vulnerability. Assure the bereaved these emotions are a normal part of coming to terms with a loss. Encourage grievers to deal with these feelings by openly discussing them. Author Robert DiGiulio, Ph.D., recalls the year when a state trooper told him a car accident had taken the lives of his wife, their oldest daughter and his wife's parents. He was hit by a flood of emotions. "I discovered it does no good to fight such feelings," he wrote. "Pushing them down only makes them come back with a greater fury. Instead, I had to learn to respect those feelings as part of me—a testament to my intense love and loss. Only when I was able to accept and even embrace such feelings as a natural, normal and integral part of my healing process was I able to work through them."

6. Resist any temptation to recite clichés. They serve only to minimize the sense of loss. When responding to comments expressed by the bereaved, use short sentences to validate their feelings and convey your care and compassion. Some examples are, "I'm sorry," "This must be very painful for you," "What can I do?" "I am concerned and want to help," "Please call me at anytime," and "May I check in with you frequently?"

One woman who experienced two miscarriages within a short period of time says, "I received all kinds of advice and most of it was useless." She advises, "Suppress any temptation to say, 'It was for the best,' 'It wasn't meant to be,' 'At least you can get pregnant again,' or 'You're young, you can try again.' And definitely don't say, 'There was probably something wrong with the baby. This is nature's way.'"

7. Make specific invitations. It helps the bereaved when friends move beyond the general statement, "Let me know how I can help," by taking the initiative and extending specific invitations. Invite them to attend a concert or a sports event with you. When planning a dinner party, remember a grieving friend might welcome an evening out. Be persistent. "If your friend refuses, call again on another occasion," says Delores Kuenning in her book, *Helping People Through Grief*. "Suggest things you can do together. Even if you simply go for a walk together, such contact will help relieve the loneliness and initiate socialization."

8. Urge caution concerning hasty decisions. Sometimes the bereaved are tempted to sell their house, move out of state, take a new job or make a major investment shortly after a death. Unless absolutely necessary, all major decisions and changes should be postponed during the first year following a loss. The bereaved need to accrue time and distance from the loss in order to gain a balanced perspective. Brothers experienced additional sadness over a decision she made too soon after her husband's death. "I regret that a few weeks after Milt died I sold his big farm tractor to a neighbor, thinking I would never need it. I regret not keeping it and learning to operate it so every time I used it, Milt's memory would have ridden along with me."

Helping the Bereaved to Heal

Remember that your gentle support is vital for the bereaved to experience peace and healing in the place of pain and hurting. With the help of kind friends, the grieving can take on a new direction in their lives and once again experience the joy of living.

Talking to Children About Grief and Death

Joy Johnson

An expert on bereavement, Joy Johnson is the cofounder of the Centering Corporation in Omaha, Nebraska, the oldest bereavement resource center in the United States. In the following selection, Johnson explains that children may not understand death fully and therefore experience grief differently than adults do. For this reason, she states, it is important for adults to learn how to help children through the grieving process. Johnson suggests several strategies for talking to children about death, depending on their age level. She stresses that, while it is not easy, adults must be honest with children about the realities of death. She also points out that children may respond to death in ways that adults find discomforting, such as using black humor; adults need to realize that these reactions are normal for children, she writes. If necessary, Johnson advises, adults should be prepared to ask for professional assistance in helping children to cope with the death of a loved one.

We would protect them if we could. We would take away the hurt, but we can't. As much as we would like to pretend they don't understand, they do. Children grieve. And how they grieve throughout a lifetime depends greatly on how we teach them about death, involve them in family rituals of grieving, and guide them through their grief. How we tell them, what we say, and how we act around death have a tremendous impact on them. It is easy to ignore questions. It is easy to assume that children think as we do. But they don't, and sometimes their logic can be amazing.

Once, when a little girl was crying over the death of her cat, her mother tried to comfort her. "Don't worry, honey," she explained. "Your cat is with God in heaven." The little girl looked at her mother, her eyes widening. "What does God want with a dead cat?" she asked.

It is important to explain death to children, starting at a very early age. Our granddaughter, Paris, was stung by a bee when she was two.

Joy Johnson, "Talking to Children About Grief and Death," *Mothering*, January 1998, p. 72.

After that, she pointed at and named every insect "Beee! Beee!" Then one day she and I came across a dead bee lying on the sidewalk. "Beee!" Paris said, pointing.

"Dead bee," I said, "Dead. Dead. See, the bee doesn't move now." I picked it up. It lay on its back, its little legs in the air. Paris stared. "The bee can't feel now. Dead," I said again.

Paris put one tiny finger on the small wing. "Dead," she whispered. Even at age two she had somehow picked up my seriousness about the state of the one-time stinger. Her one whispered word said she knew deep down that this was important. Something very unique had happened to that bee.

Children do not naturally fear death. We instill it in them, put a black shroud around it, and worry it into power. But when we really look at death and what it means, it takes on a dramatically different appearance. One of our friends, David Prowse, played Darth Vader in the *Star Wars* trilogy. There is no more frightening symbol of death and destruction than the powerful lord of the dark side. Yet, if you get to know David, he will tell you that as soon as his helmet was put over his head, his breath fogged up the goggles. The costume was extremely heavy. When he began to walk, his pants fell down. Throughout the films he wore suspenders to keep Darth Vader's shorts from showing. Once we become acquainted with death, we realize it can't see all that well and that its pants may fall down, too.

Guidelines for Talking to Children

There are several things to keep in mind as you explain death and grief to children.

Be Honest. Children are people readers. If you try to fake them out, you'll eventually get caught, and it won't be pleasant. One grandmother told us that her daughter had committed suicide. She had refused to tell her six-year-old grandson how his mother died. We asked a very important question, "Would you rather he hear it from you, knowing that you love him and will be there to answer questions, or do you want him to hear it from a classmate during a moment of childhood cruelty, or to overhear it during a family get-together?" If the child discovers the truth either way, he's likely to feel betrayed, left out, not-to-be-trusted, and deeply hurt.

"But how can I talk about such a terrible thing to a little boy?" the grandmother asked. She ended up going home, taking him on her lap, and saying, "Tony, there's something I want you to know, and I want you to hear it from me because I love you and I'm here to answer your questions. Your mommy's mind was very, very sick. She wanted to die and couldn't think clearly. She killed herself and thought that would solve her problems. She didn't know it wouldn't solve anything, and she didn't know how sad it would make us." Grandma began to cry. Tony began to cry. They held each other. Now

Tony can ask the questions he needs to ask, and Grandma doesn't have to waste the horrendous amount of energy it takes to keep the skeleton in the closet.

Be Prepared to Meet Resistance. My Aunt Bess never wanted a child to know the truth. "Why do you want to put him through this?" she said when we insisted that our two-year-old son attend his grandfather's funeral. "Tell him some story. Make something up." Later I saw her holding Jim. "See how Grandpa is asleep?" she said, pointing to the figure of my dad in the casket.

Jim was almost three. I didn't want him avoiding his afternoon nap thinking he might end up in a casket, unable to move. We looked at some of the flowers that had arrived at the funeral almost dead. "Look," I said. "These are dead. Grandpa is dead, too. He's not asleep. He won't ever come back, and we'll never see him again. We'll always remember him, and we'll always love him, and we'll remember that he loved us, too, but he is dead, not asleep."

Jim reached out and touched his grandfather's hand. He shook his head. "No, not asleep," he said. Remember, there's nothing frightening or creepy about a body. If you've never touched one, put this magazine down and rub the cover. That's what it feels like.

Questions About God's Will

Another element of resistance you may meet is the "God's will" talk. This is a real comfort to some people but not necessarily to children. "God came and took Daddy" is about as frightening as you can get! We encourage sharing your personal beliefs and at the same time being careful no one makes God into a parent-, grandparent-, or child-snatcher.

When you hear someone expressing this idea, you might want to handle it like Amy, a young mom whose seven year old, Timmy, died. Timmy's brother, Jason, was four. She explained carefully that Timmy had died, and then, expressing their beliefs, she explained that after Timmy died, God had come and taken his soul—the part of Timmy that loved and laughed and was. That part, she explained, was gone now. What was left was just Timmy's body, like a peanut shell with no peanut, like a schoolhouse with no children.

She did a good job. Jason understood. Two days after the funeral, Jason climbed on Mom's lap. "Mom, God came and got Timmy's soul, right?"

"Right, Jason."

"Well, why didn't you wake me up?" Jason exclaimed.

"I just didn't think about it, Jason. There were people here to get Tim's body, and in all the rush, I didn't think about it. I'm sorry. Why did you want to be awakened?"

"I wanted to see God!" Jason said. "What was God drivin', anyhow?"

Be Real. Let your children know that families who love each other laugh together and cry together. Tell your child it's OK to cry and it's OK for you to cry, too. One little girl, Heather, only 21 months old, refused to talk about her nine-month-old sister who had died. She would not even say Jessica's name. A sensitive friend pointed out that Heather talked about Jess and asked questions when she was with her, but every time she mentioned Jess at home, both parents began to cry. Heather taught us that even very young children protect others from tears.

Heather's daddy took her into Jess's room and sat with her in the rocking chair. He told her it was all right to talk about Jess any time she wanted to. He told her it was all right when he and Mommy cried—that they would be sad for a long, long time, but they were still a family.

"You don't have to be afraid of our tears," Daddy said. "It helps to cry, and it helps to talk about Jess."

"Jessica!" Heather squealed. "Jessica! Jessica! Jessica!" And she ran into the living room and started looking at Jessica's pictures and talking about Jess. It was a powerful release for a small child.

Age-Appropriate Discussions

Respect the Age of Your Child. Even a newborn will pick up on your body language and your emotions. If you are tight from stress and grief, your baby will feel it through your arms, hear it in your voice. Parents have reported increased crying in very young infants during times of grief. It's as if they are insisting you notice that they're a part of the family, too.

• Infant to Age Three. Children this age cannot understand the finality of death. They can comprehend that the dead person cannot feel anything, does not breathe in and out anymore. They can understand that the person can no longer eat or go to the bathroom. They may not be very sad because they think the person is coming back. "When are we going to pick up Jess?" Heather asked months after her sister died. Each time her mother explained that Jess wasn't coming back. When Heather wanted to draw pictures to send to Jess, her parents let her mail them. Gradually, Heather grew into the notion of permanence. Three year olds may not grasp the full concept of death, but they do understand sadness. It's important to tell them why you are sad; to let them know that sadness is a part of feeling when someone dies, and that even though you are sad, there are times when you will laugh. You may want to tell your child that when you are sad, you need a hug. This gives the child something helpful to do.

• Three to Six. While death isn't permanent yet to children this age, they are making connections. Now we get to explain that there's sick, very sick, and very, very sick. "I don't want Mommy and Daddy to leave me anymore," Rachael said.

"Oh?" I said, giving my favorite dynamic response to a kid statement like this.

"Yeah," she replied. "The last time they left me alone, Grandma died." Her parents had gone to a play, leaving Rachael with a babysitter. When they came home, there was a message to call Grandma's house. Grandma had died unexpectedly, and Rachael made the connection.

"Dead means you get run over by a train and then get up again," Jon told us. His favorite cartoon was Roadrunner. With children this age, it's most important to share your tears, give permission to cry, and allow play. Remember, kids don't think in a linear manner. They will play, then grieve; grieve, then play. Frankly, we could probably learn a lot from their style of sorrow.

• Six to Nine. At this stage, kids are into details. "How did he die? . . . Who killed him?" Children this age see death as someone or something that comes and gets you. They think they can catch it. They, like us, become scared. If the death is violent, children are not only victimized, they're traumatized. Even a long illness can bring out the fear that someone else close to them will die. It's time to share details of the death, to explain the difference between cancer and an earache. As children age, they'll want more details. Nine year olds may be satisfied with "Aunt Liz's heart was very weak. It finally stopped. It's not at all like your healthy young heart." Thirteen year olds want to know if Aunt Liz had a heart attack, heart disease, or heartbreak.

• Ten Through Teens. Children in this age group have feelings that are similar to those of adults. They want details, and often they will use black humor or attempt to "gross you out" with death jokes or overly vivid descriptions. We're likely to see more anger and more acting out from this age group. Teens may withdraw or risk death to prove they're invincible, throwing parents into panic and despair. Sharon Turnbull, who wrote *Who Lives Happily Ever After?* about violent death, says you must approach a teen as you would a deer: quietly, softly, slowly.

Do not assume teenagers can handle grief alone. They can't. Even if they're distant and don't want to listen, talk about how you feel, your fears, your needs and expectations. Provide a journal or blank notebook so they can write down feelings, copy lyrics, or create poems. An excellent resource is the Centering Corporation's journal for teens, *Fire in My Heart: Ice in My Veins.* Also tell teachers and school counselors that your teen may need extra attention.

Guilt and Regret

Be Ready for Guilt. Make sure your child knows he or she did not cause the death. When Kisha's sister died, the seven year old suddenly stopped speaking. At last she told a very patient bereavement counselor that just before her sister was hit by a car, Kisha had yelled, "You should be dead! I hate you. Go away." It took some convincing before Kisha really believed that her words and thoughts couldn't make anyone die.

If your child is older, you might want to talk about the difference between guilt and regret. Guilt is what we feel when we deliberately, consciously, intentionally hurt or do harm. Regret is what we feel when we wish we could have done something to prevent hurt or harm. Every child, no matter what age, needs to know he or she didn't make it happen.

Know You Don't Have to Do Everything Alone. Ask for help. If you want counseling, ask if the counselor knows anything about grief. Talk to teachers, school counselors, your funeral director, and your minister. If you are active in a church or synagogue, talk with your rabbi or clergy. Read everything you can find on bereavement. Ask about support groups and centers for grieving children.

A Rich Experience

Grief is love's sorrow. As soon as children know love, they prepare to know grief. It is only in the last ten years that we have come to truly recognize the needs of grieving children and the need of all children to know about death. Death is one of the most important issues of life. You don't remember your birth, but you may be very aware of your approaching death. Sharing feelings honestly with your children removes the tremendous burden of taking care of everyone else. Sharing information about death allows your children to know you are there for questions and are not afraid of honest answers. Death and the grief that follows may not be a pleasant experience, but it can be a very, very rich one.

CHAPTER 4

ETHICAL ISSUES AT THE END OF LIFE

The Ethical Obligation to Consider the Spiritual Needs of the Dying

John Hardwig

John Hardwig is the head of the philosophy department at the University of Tennessee in Knoxville, where he specializes in bioethics. He is also the author of the book *Is There a Duty to Die? And Other Essays in Bioethics*. In the following selection, Hardwig maintains that the spiritual needs of the dying are not being met by the medical establishment, which tends to focus solely on the physical aspects of end-of-life care. In order for people to experience a truly good death, Hardwig believes, this neglect of their spiritual needs must be remedied. In fact, the author asserts, impending deaths should not be handled primarily by doctors but by people trained to treat deaths as the spiritual events they are. He suggests that bioethicists should take an active role in meeting the spiritual concerns of dying patients, helping them to face the end of life with purpose and dignity.

When I am dying, I am quite sure that the central issues for me will not be whether I am put on a ventilator, whether CPR is attempted when my heart stops, or whether I receive artificial feeding. Although each of these could be important, each will almost certainly be quite peripheral. Rather, my central concerns will be how to face my death, how to bring my life to a close, and how best to help my family go on without me. A ventilator will not help me do these things—not unless all I need is a little more time to get the job done.

Unfortunately, however, bioethics has succumbed to the agendas of physicians. Physicians face ethical concerns about treatment decisions—when to offer, withhold, and withdraw various treatments—and treatment decisions have been the focus of bioethics as well. But the issues that most trouble patients and their families at the end of life are not these. To them, the end of life is a spiritual crisis.

The word "spiritual" is ambiguous. As I use it, spiritual refers to concerns about the ultimate meaning and values in life. It has to do

John Hardwig, "Spiritual Issues at the End of Life: A Call for Discussion," *Hastings Center Report*, vol. 30, March 2000, pp. 28–33.

with our deepest sense of who we are and what life is all about. Spiritual does not imply any belief in a supreme being or in a life after this. Atheists have spiritual concerns just like everyone else.

Spiritual, then, does not mean religious. Indeed, this sense of spiritual forces us to ask, How effectively do organized religions address the spiritual needs of their members? It may be that some organized religions—or some representatives of them—serve to silence spiritual concerns at the end of life or to distract people from them. Certainly many American churches do not talk much about death and dying. One minister confessed, "We talk a lot about what we believe comes after death. But we skip pretty quickly over dying itself, except to say to make your peace with the Lord." Often, there are strong social and religious pressures to suppress any doubts or questions; doubts and questions are taken as a sign of a weak faith. As a result, Christians can still find that their faith gives them no guidance about how to live the final chapter of life.

What the Dying Suffer From

People facing death suffer from an inability to find meaning in this last chapter of their lives; from a bleak, narrowly confined and abbreviated future; from inability to deal meaningfully with family and loved ones at this final opportunity; from total dependence on others; from loss of capabilities; from being turned from a contributor into a burden on others; from the indignity of being unable to take care of even basic bodily functions; from a sense that their bodies or their minds are betraying them; from being cast out of the world in which the healthy live; from guilt; from a sense of abandonment; from anger about all of this; and from isolation due to the reluctance of the healthy to broach the subject of dying.

These are all spiritual issues, or at least quickly bring spiritual questions into view. Facing death brings to the surface questions about what life is all about. Long-buried assumptions and commitments are revealed. And many find that the beliefs and values they have lived by no longer seem valid or do not sustain them. These are the ingredients of a spiritual crisis, the stuff of spiritual suffering.

Yet they are not the themes of bioethics. Some will object that they are not properly themes of ethics at all, but if they are the dominant concerns of dying patients, bioethics has failed to address patients' concerns at the end of life. This failure has ramifications throughout the discipline of bioethics.

Spirituality and Bioethics

1. Many patients show little interest in making treatment decisions. "What difference does it make?" one patient told her doctor. She was not asking: her tone and expression made it clear that any difference a treatment decision could make would not be important to her now.

Advance directives and the entire theory of proxy decisions are also largely irrelevant to patient concerns at the end of life. They too focus on treatment. Indeed, it is possible that one reason so many people do not complete advance directives is precisely this irrelevance: I expect it will hardly matter to me what kind of treatment I receive when I am unable even to recognize myself or my loved ones.

Yet when patients and especially families struggle with treatment decisions, the struggle is often rooted in the questions' spiritual dimensions.

2. Giving pain and analgesia too central a place in the care of the dying could easily distort end of life care. Relief of pain is clearly important. However, better management of pain will do nothing to ease the suffering brought on by the specter of my end, the indignity of my decline and debility, the prospect of useless and purposeless days lying in the hospital bed, the emptiness and darkness of my future.

3. Similarly, the entire discussion of physician-assisted suicide threatens to become skewed by an inordinate focus on the pain of terminal illness. Requests for physician-assisted suicide are not motivated simply by pain or fear of pain. Death is horrible not primarily because it is painful, and my fear of death is not primarily fear of pain. (I may have experienced worse pain before.) It is a spiritual crisis that motivates many requests for physician-assisted suicide.

4. Aging, chronic illness, and nursing home care are all harbingers of death. We Americans avoid them, dislike them, dislike even thinking of them partly for that reason. Of course, each brings its own forms of spiritual suffering as well.

5. Families suffer too. They face the impending loss of a loved one with the difficulty of imagining how to go on without her. Loss of a loved one is normally also a spiritual crisis: family members may well have to reshape their identities and redefine their basic commitments when their loved one is gone. Long unresolved family issues threaten to become permanently unresolvable. Family consensus often proves elusive. And the family too suffers from guilt and from a sense of abandonment. Physicians relate stories about distant family members who suddenly materialize when dad or mom is dying and vehemently insist that everything be done. The common view is that their demand for aggressive treatment is fueled by guilt and by a desire to atone for past neglect. But guilt and atonement are spiritual issues.

6. Thus perhaps many requests for futile treatment reflect the fact that patients and their families have not completed the essential human tasks of dying. The inability to "let go" may express an inability to complete relationships as much as love for a dying family member. In any case, love too requires an ability to let go, as Simone Weil somewhere reminds us: "in loving, we need to learn only how to let go; holding comes naturally."

The Bioethical Silence

I submit, then, that patient and family issues at the end of life are almost entirely spiritual, for perhaps especially at the end of life, we become aware that we are spiritual beings. These would be important common denominators of our difficulties with dying, a central element in adequate care for the dying.

Why have contemporary bioethicists been so largely silent about spiritual issues at the end of life? It is partly because they have conceived of bioethics as an ethics for physicians and other health care professionals. Despite all the emphasis on patient autonomy and patient empowerment, the responsibilities on which bioethicists focus are the responsibilities of physicians and other health professionals. We have had virtually nothing to say about the responsibilities of autonomous patients, certainly nothing at all to say about how to die a responsible death.

Bioethicists' silence may also be due partly to the fact we have been struggling to establish bioethics as a secular discipline. We badly want a place at the table in secular health care institutions. We want to speak to scientifically minded physicians and to distinguish ourselves from chaplains and other clergy.

Bioethicists have also struggled to present a unified face and a unified theory to the world of health care. A unified body of knowledge and perspective bolster our claim to professional status. Spiritual issues may well divide us. Perhaps we also fear the depth and intractability of dissension over spiritual issues, as well as the dogmatism that can so easily be aroused by it.

Finally, bioethics may be hamstrung by the contemporary assumption that ethics is solely about right and wrong conduct. However unable a patient may have been to bring her life to a successful close, it would be very odd to say she died wrong. But ethics is more than a theory of right and wrong conduct, and bioethics must surely be more. A bad death is not necessarily or even primarily a "wrong death" or the result of a series of "unethical" decisions at the end of life. A bad death is also a meaningless death, or one marked by an inability to accept one's mortality, or one that is divisive and destructive to loved ones and families. Thus if good care for the dying is a part of bioethics, we cannot avoid these spiritual issues.

Even more basically, a discussion of spiritual issues at the end of life is central to ethics in the classic sense, in which a pivotal question is, What is the good life? Such an ethics teaches how to live, and so also how to die. I suggest a return to older traditions in which it made sense for an ethicist to offer a manual on how to die. Such an ethics offers advice or counsel, not prohibitions and injunctions. If a label is helpful, the discussion I intend would be one part of a "eudaemonistic bioethics." [Eudaemonism is the theory that the highest ethical goal is personal well-being and happiness.]

Care of the Dying

The theoretical silence of bioethicists is reflected in a practical neglect. Health care institutions generally do little to help patients and families deal with the spiritual issues of the end of life. At most, they provide a chaplaincy service to which such questions can be handed off. But spiritual issues must not be left to chaplains or other clergy, helpful as they often are, for that leaves unmet the spiritual concerns of those who do not share the faith commitments of the chaplains' religions. Also, a service available only at the end of life may be too late. The spiritual suffering at the end of life may begin well before the patient is actively dying. Once, people normally got sick and died in a matter of days or weeks. Now the average American will know three years in advance what she will die of. Even a terminal illness is not always necessary; aging alone also brings with it a recognition that death is no longer remote.

Should we expect physicians to assist terminally ill patients in dealing with spiritual issues, too? There seems to be a variety of reasons not to. Aren't physicians too focused on diseases? Aren't the medical treatment issues themselves complicated and vexing enough? Do physicians have either the disposition or training that would enable them to help patients deal with the end of their lives? After all, physicians are reported to have an unusually high death anxiety that medical school does little to alleviate. The role of a physician is already overwhelmingly complex. Wouldn't asking physicians also to take on the role of spiritual counselor at the end of life prove to be both unrealistic and unsustainable? Moreover, the bewildering array of unfamiliar medical specialists that patients face at the end of life would fragment any spiritual care beyond usefulness, and the cost-containment pressures that are forcing physicians to spend less and less time with any one patient perhaps effectively prohibit serious attention to spiritual concerns.

But if physicians are not suited for the job, then we ought to "demedicalize" death. We ought not put doctors in charge of the care of the terminally ill. Doctors should be "ancillary personnel," for their expertise is just too peripheral to the concerns of the dying. The hospice movement has taken steps in that direction, but the care of a much broader spectrum of dying patients would need to be removed from the hands of physicians. Spiritual care is the core of care for the dying.

A Nonreligious, Spiritual Discussion

I believe we must move the discussion of spiritual issues at the end of life to center stage in bioethics. The discussion must be, in large part at least, an inclusive, nonreligious discussion. We need such an inclusive discussion because the spiritual needs of the unreligious must also be met. For nontheists, only a nonreligious discussion can hope to articulate the spiritual needs of a secular world. Also, for members of religious communities, only a nonreligious discussion can lay bare the concerns and mind set of our contemporary culture, revealing the spiritual issues at the end of life that even religious discussions will have to address. Further, strong religious convictions are not sufficient to ensure a good death or to endow the terminal phase of life with meaning, purpose, or validity. My eighty-eight-year-old mother is absolutely convinced that she will be reunited with her husband in heaven, but she says to me over and over again, "John, why does this have to take so long?"

Only at the end of such a discussion will we know whether there are spiritual common denominators shared by all or many of the dying. Only then will we be able to locate the pivotal differences. Only a serious effort at such discussion will determine whether we can talk with each other across the differences in our religious convictions.

The Need to Reform Hospice Care Regulations

Jennifer G. Hickey

Hospice care is designed to provide terminally ill patients with pain relief while forgoing intrusive medical procedures, enabling those in the last stages of dying to spend their final days in peace. According to Jennifer G. Hickey, a staff writer for the weekly magazine *Insight on the News*, government regulations have made it increasingly more difficult for patients to rely on hospice care. Since 1997, hospice stays subsidized by Medicare have a limit of six months, she explains; if patients live longer than six months, the hospice providers face huge fines for abusing the Medicare payment program. Hickey maintains that this time limit gives hospice providers an incentive to reject prospective patients who might not die within six months. Concerned that many patients who need compassionate care are not receiving it, she states, some medical professionals have proposed that the six-month rule be eliminated or amended to allow more flexibility in the time limitation.

In 1997 the U.S. Supreme Court ruled unanimously that terminally ill people do not have a constitutional right to doctor-assisted suicide, thus upholding laws in New York and Washington state.

But the issue of end-of-life care still burns in the national dialogue. The debate was reignited when CBS' *60 Minutes* decided to air video of Jack Kevorkian's controversial assist in the suicide of a man with Lou Gehrig's disease. But the narrow focus on Kevorkian and his efforts to legalize the termination of life diminishes the work of another community in America that has been working since 1977 to bring dignity to the terminally ill through hospice and alternative end-of-life care.

The word "hospice" derives from the same linguistic root as "hospitality." It began as a medieval practice of providing shelter and aid to weary and ill travelers and has developed into a large network of at-home and inpatient services to comfort the terminally ill and their families. "Hospice isn't a place. It's a type of care that is compassionate and meets the medical, personal and spiritual needs," says H. James Towey, president of the Commission on Aging with Dignity. "It has to do with dignity."

The Origins of Hospice

Hospice offers palliative care—pain relief without active measures for a cure—for individuals in the final stages of disease. Approximately 65 percent of hospices are nonprofit; 4 percent are government organizations, according to the National Hospice Organization, or NHO. A 1995 NHO census shows that 60 percent of hospice patients suffer from cancer and 4 percent from AIDS. One in four non-sudden deaths occur in hospice.

The modern hospice originated in 1967 when Dame Cicely Saunders founded St. Christopher's Hospice in a London suburb. Saunders brought the idea to the United States during a lecture series she conducted in 1963 and in subsequent visits during the 1960s. However, it was during the 1970s that hospice began to get its foothold.

During a 1972 session of the Senate Special Committee on Aging, bereavement expert Elisabeth Kübler-Ross testified, "We live in a very particular death-denying society. We isolate both the dying and the old, and it serves a purpose. They are reminders of our own mortality." Two years later, Idaho Sens. Frank Church and Frank E. Moss introduced legislation to provide federal funding for hospice care. While the effort did not succeed, the same year would witness the establishment of the first hospice.

By 1979, the Health Care Financing Administration would opt to earmark federal funds for demonstration programs at 26 hospices around the country. But it was when Congress included a provision to create a Medicare hospice benefit in the Tax Equity and Fiscal Responsibility Act of 1982 and made the benefit permanent in 1986 that hospice became an accepted division of the health-care field.

Approximately 3,200 hospice programs operate or are planned in all 50 states and the District of Columbia, according to the NHO. Modern hospice brings in nurses, physicians, therapists, social workers and volunteers; the aim is to keep families involved in all of the decision-making processes.

The years from 1993 to 1998 have seen an annual 17 percent growth in hospices. A 1997 evaluation of the Medicare hospice benefit found that for every dollar spent on hospice care, $1.26 was saved by Medicare. Hospice is a benefit under many private insurance plans, health maintenance organizations and managed-care programs, as well as Medicare. The federal government, through the Medicare program, pays for three-quarters of hospice care. Although Medicare spent $1.9 billion on hospice in 1995, it amounted to only 1 percent of the Medicare budget. Medicare provides for reimbursement in all 50 states; Medicaid reimburses for hospice care in 42 states.

An Incentive for Death?

But with government involvement has come unending regulatory red tape and episodes of purported abuse. As a result of regulations written into the Balanced Budget Act of 1997, patients must be within six months of death to be admitted to hospice. In addition, a patient or the patient's family must provide two letters from their doctors attesting to the terminal nature of their illness and the patient's understanding that active curative care must be forgone. The regulation is intended to prevent use of hospice by persons who should be in other programs. But does the regulation give hospice providers an incentive to hope for death?

In cases in which an individual survives past six months, the federal government fines the hospice $50,000 for perpetrating abuse of the program. Since 1995, according to an Office of the Inspector General report, only 15 percent of those admitted nationwide survive more than six months. But pockets of abuse do occur. A 1997 review of hospice facilities in four states found that 65.1 percent of patients participating weren't terminally ill, resulting in $83 million in inappropriate payments. One Florida hospice was fined $8.9 million, wiping out its profits for five years, because 176 of its 15,426 dying patients lived too long. "That is a complete misuse of hospice to get the benefit of hospice," says Towey, responding to allegations of non-terminally ill individuals entering hospice.

The unintended result is that operators of nonprofit hospices fear they will be obliged to reimburse the costs in cases which are disputed. Therefore, some are less willing to take in patients who are not dying quickly enough. Most cancer patients in a terminal stage die in less than six months. However, among patients with AIDS, congestive heart failure and a few other illnesses, judgments of the length of terminal state are more difficult to make.

Government Intrusion

One such case that illustrates the sometimes pernicious incentives of government regulation is that of Virginia residents Frederic Andres and his 100-year-old mother, Frances. Frances Andres entered hospice in Loudoun County, Va., on Feb. 20, 1998, after suffering a mild stroke which left her with temporary partial paralysis on the right side of her mouth and her right leg.

Andres, the former vice chairman of the Interstate Commerce Commission in the Reagan administration, was pleased with the work of the volunteers who were visiting and caring for his mother. However, he wanted to restructure the care his mother had been receiving and asked the hospice for a so-called "timeout." While discussions were ongoing, an unidentified informant charged that Andres was "criminally negligent" in the care of his mother by removing her from hospice. The county's Adult Protective Services, or APS, then was brought into the case and attempted to interview Mrs. Andres to determine whether she was being mistreated, an action APS says it was compelled by law to take.

Believing that APS' request was intrusive and a violation of his mother's Fourth Amendment rights, Andres balked at the request. In addition to being concerned about the aggressive involvement of APS, Andres—a former regional director for the American Medical Association—became concerned about the six-month regulatory deadline the federal government imposes on hospice care. "I did not know that hospice was meant to preside over death," Andres says.

County Supervisor Steven D. Whitener wrote to APS, pleading with them to call an end to their action against the Andreses, adding, "This issue is not about the care and well-being of Mrs. Andres. It's about the government getting paid, and billable hours for social services [of APS]."

But the struggle took a dramatic turn when Andres learned that the county was attempting to have a court-appointed guardian assigned to his mother. He decided to move his mother to Canada to gain asylum. While on the road, he learned that a social worker claimed in court (falsely) that Andres was carrying a weapon, that an all-points-bulletin was calling for his arrest and, according to exaggerated statements by county officials, his mother was near death because of his actions to protect her from government intrusion.

Andres' prime complaint was the involvement of the social-services department and its attempt, in his mind, to violate his constitutional rights to due process, security against unreasonable search and seizure and the right to confront accusers in court. While acknowledging the beneficial efforts of the hospice volunteers and the generally accepted reputation of hospice as a respite for the ill, Andres contemptuously calls the social workers "simply hitmen for the federal government." However, despite all of the media attention, legal wrangling and burdensome costs to the Andreses, not to mention the taxpayers, Frances Andres recently turned 101 years old, living peacefully with her son in their new home in Okeechobee, Fla.

Making Changes

However, changes in the 20-year program are being proposed. One would be to allow patients to leave hospice if an improvement occurs and to return with no penalty if a downturn occurs. Second, some health-care professionals are leaning toward the retraction of the six-month rule.

One of the biggest areas of discussion in end-of-life issues is the Medicare-imposed six-month-stay regulation. Towey believes that hospice would be better served by allowing patients to be admitted while undergoing active curative care. "I would like to pursue the curative route until there is no chance of recovery."

Paul Stander, medical director of Good Samaritan Regional Medical Center in Phoenix echoes this sentiment. "We doctors who are honest about it admit that we aren't very good at predicting how much time a person has to live." In fact, some medical professionals are courting the idea of allowing patients to enter hospice while they are still receiving curative care.

With a $450,000 grant from the Robert Wood Johnson Foundation, Hospice of the Valley in Phoenix has made such a move. "Phoenix-Care" will provide palliative care for patients over the final three years of life.

Towey believes that the more Americans learn, the more hospice will be seen as the most compassionate way to die or to care for the terminally ill. While acknowledging that improvements and reforms should be made in its development, he clarifies the primary draw and function of hospice. "When you look at Kevorkian, you would think the only choice is pain or prison. What we have lost at the end of life is that softness, that touch. That is what hospice care is all about."

Ensuring Adequate Pain Management for the Dying

Nancy Stedman

Many people unnecessarily suffer from severe pain before they die, Nancy Stedman writes in the following selection. She reports that most doctors do not like to offer dying patients strong pain relievers such as morphine for fear of being charged with overprescribing addictive drugs. In addition, Stedman finds, patients can be reluctant to ask for stronger medication because they do not want to appear weak or untrusting of their physicians. However, some Americans are beginning to demand the right to a pain-free death: As an example, the author relates the story of the Bergman family, who won a civil suit against their father's doctor for neglecting to provide adequate pain management during his final days. According to Stedman, the Bergman case has set a precedent that has encouraged more doctors to begin addressing pain-management issues. Stedman is a New York–based freelance writer whose work has appeared in many national publications.

Bill Bergman was a man of few words and many scruples—the sort who didn't like to draw attention to himself. And so he probably would have been mortified to hear that, after his intensely painful death, he starred in a landmark lawsuit that would eventually help protect other aging patients from suffering a similar fate.

Family Matters

A gun-toting detective for 37 years at Western Pacific Railroad, the handsome Scandinavian-American worked close by his much-adored wife, Barbara, a payroll employee and union vice president for the same company. Together, in the Northern California town of Hayward, they raised three children: Beverly, now 46, the peacemaker of the family; Robert, 41, the clown with a melancholy streak; and Alice, 51, the iconoclast who always maintained a measure of independence from her family.

Bill was often eclipsed by his funny and vivacious wife. "My mother

Nancy Stedman, "A Father's Death, a Daughter's Legacy," *Health*, vol. 16, May 2002, pp. 130–35.

was like the biggest thing in the room," recalls Bev, an advocate for mentally ill people who now lives in the same home where she and her siblings grew up. "My father was very quiet. He would just sit in the background and let my mom be right out there." Away from the job, Bill tended to pursue solitary pleasures. "He loved to putter around the house," Bev adds. "He would paint anything that stayed still."

It was only after their mom's death from lung cancer in 1995, though, that Bev, Robert, and Alice got to know their father: that he had only gone to baseball games to please his wife, that he was an opera fan. The more the kids learned about their father, the closer they grew to him during the three years before his death. "He was always good about telling us he loved us," Bev says, "but he got a lot more huggy in the last few years."

So it was especially sad for the siblings when their dad passed away in 1998. But what made Bill's death more than a tragic family loss was the fact that he had spent his final week in excruciating pain. Bill's suffering—by almost all accounts unnecessary—led Beverly and her siblings to bring and win an elder-abuse lawsuit against his physician for inadequate pain management, the first suit of its kind in the United States.

Equally important, the case helped spark legislative remedies for families who believe that their loved one's pain is being undertreated by a doctor—a disturbingly common problem. According to one recent report, half of all terminally ill patients in the United States experience moderate to severe pain. The Bergman case also sent a message to doctors across the nation, one they clearly got: Anecdotal reports suggest that in the wake of the case, physicians are signing up for pain-management courses in increasing numbers. The distress of one quiet man was heard 'round the medical world.

The Caretaker

By her own reckoning, Beverly Bergman inherited her social activism from her mother and her bulldog persistence from her father. She spent much of the 1980s protesting the building of nuclear power plants in her native California. A naturally reserved woman whose face can light up unexpectedly with a smile—or with outrage at a social or personal injustice—she was a peer drug counselor in high school and made her career in social services. "She's always been a very shirt-off-your-back kind of person," says her brother, Robert. And he should know. A heavy drinker for years, he turned to her in 1988 when his problem got out of control. "I probably wouldn't be alive today if she had not been there," he says. "She drove me to the detox center. She was with me the whole time and helped me get sober."

Bev, the only sibling without children, also took over the care of her mother after she was diagnosed with terminal lung cancer. Bev set up a hospital bed in her own apartment and arranged for hospice nurses and home health aides during the workday. After two months, her mother died at Bev's home. "She had a very peaceful death," Bev says.

Not so for her dad. The longest nine days in Bev's life began in mid-February 1998, when she discovered her father crumpled over in a kitchen chair, unable to move. "I'm in terrible pain," whispered Bill, who was not inclined to show weakness. He was rushed to the emergency room of nearby Eden Medical Center, a 275-bed hospital in Castro Valley. The next day, an E.R. physician gave Bill two small doses of morphine, the drug of choice for severe pain, according to guidelines issued by the U.S. Agency for Health Care Policy and Research. It was the last morphine, the last shred of relief, Bill Bergman would receive until just before he died.

Enduring Terrible Suffering

The internist who took over his case, Wing Chin, M.D., a former chief of staff at the medical center, admitted Bill to the hospital and ordered low doses of Demerol, a much weaker painkiller. And since it was prescribed on an as-needed basis, Bill had to wait until he was extremely uncomfortable before getting relief. His medical charts tell the horrific tale: His discomfort ranged mostly between 7 and 10 (the most excruciating level of pain).

Doctors diagnosed Bill with compressed vertebrae, but the family suspected lung cancer was the real cause of pain for their father, a longtime smoker. Bill's initial tests for lung cancer were inconclusive, and he declined to undergo invasive tests for a definitive diagnosis. Nevertheless, he became convinced he was going to die, and wanted to be at home when it happened. He was released from the hospital on Saturday, and Bev moved back into the family's home to take care of him. She was shocked to learn that Chin had only prescribed Vicodin, a moderate pain reliever. It wasn't powerful enough: Bev could hear her father moaning in pain, unable to sleep. "I'd play music to distract him," she recalls. "And it would work for a while. But then the pain would just come back."

By Monday, Bill's pain was the most intense he had ever experienced. "He was clutching on to the trapeze bars above the bed, saying how awful it was," Bev says. A sympathetic and persistent hospice nurse managed to get a prescription for liquid morphine from Bill's former family practitioner. It was not until that afternoon that he finally received a dose. "In about an hour he went to sleep," Bev says. "The next day his breathing got shallower, and he died." It was February 24, 1998, nine days after Bill first collapsed.

More than four years later, Bev still cries at the memory of those dark days. "When something happens like this, it makes you think of all the things you could have done differently," she says. "I think I was depending too much on the nurses. The first nurse who came to the house didn't call the doctor about pain medication. We're taught not to question authority, and, because nurses and doctors are the ones who went to school, they know best. But that's not really true."

Inadequate Treatment for Pain

None of us would ever want our parents to go through what Bill Bergman did. However, the chances that they could are frighteningly high. The pain-medication needs of elderly patients, who often feel reluctant about complaining to or questioning their doctors, are especially likely to be overlooked. Some 40 percent of nursing-home patients with chronic or acute pain are not receiving treatment that relieves it, according to a study published in October 2001 in *The Journal of the American Medical Association.* "There's no type of health-care institution other than the hospice that's doing a good job of pain management," says the study's lead investigator, Joan Teno, M.D., of Brown University's Center for Gerontology and Health Care Research.

Considering that there is a small armament of pain-relief medication available to the informed physician, why do so many patients seem to be losing the battle against pain? "Doctors are so worried about overprescribing for pain that we often underprescribe," says Robert Brody, M.D., chief of the Pain Consultation Clinic at San Francisco General Hospital. Part of the problem is rooted in old-fashioned American values. "Our culture tends to admire stoicism," says Linda Emanuel, M.D., Ph.D., the director of the Buehler Center on Aging at Northwestern University. Another issue is the chance of addiction. But even with morphine and other opiates, the most effective painkillers, there is only a slight risk. The American legal system has generally stressed the importance of preventing addiction over the need to relieve pain—even among terminally ill patients. In fact, some states place almost insurmountable barriers in the way of doctors who want to prescribe narcotic painkillers.

Despite the legal hurdles, the medical establishment has acknowledged the problem of insufficient pain relief—and is slowly addressing it. In 1998, the Federation of State Medical Boards, which regulates physicians, adopted a set of model guidelines for pain management. California was actually ahead of the curve. In 1994, the Medical Board of California mailed a guidebook to all state doctors, encouraging them to aggressively treat their patients' pain. And in 1997, California's legislature passed a Pain Patient's Bill of Rights, guaranteeing that all citizens had the right to be informed of, and to choose among, their pain-relief options—including narcotics. Neither of these initiatives, though, helped Bill Bergman.

Turning to the Courts

A few weeks after Bill died, Bev contacted a malpractice lawyer. She was so disturbed by watching her father suffer that she was in therapy for post-traumatic stress disorder. She told the lawyer what had happened and passed along a comment from a hospice nurse who cared for her dad that suggested Chin had a pattern of ignoring his patients' discomfort. "I wanted Dr. Chin to change his ways so other people wouldn't have to go through this," Bev explains. "I didn't want any harm to come to him. I just wanted him to become educated."

But, as it turned out, an ordinary malpractice case would not work in California: State law doesn't allow people to collect damages for pain and suffering after someone's death. A lawyer pointed Bev to Compassion in Dying Federation (CIDF), a nonprofit advocacy group in Portland, Oregon, concerned with improved end-of-life care. First, they tried to get the Medical Board of California, the regulatory agency for physicians, to discipline Chin for his failure to treat Bill Bergman prior to his death. But the board refused to take corrective action.

The next step—taking Chin to court—was much riskier, but Bev and her siblings were in lockstep on this issue. "We talked about it, and we all agreed we had to do something," Robert says. Bev, as usual, was the logical point person. Says Robert: "My sister had the fortitude to fight—she has the heart of a lion, and she has the knowledge to deal with the legal system."

Kathryn Tucker, legal director for CIDF, opted for a novel approach: to sue Chin and the Eden Medical Center in civil court for elder abuse, which requires a higher level of proof than malpractice. The chances of winning were so slim that Tucker spent weeks looking for a lawyer willing to take the job of co-counsel. She finally enlisted attorney Jim Geagan. The stakes were high for the Bergman family. If they lost the case, the Bergmans—all modest earners—would be liable for Chin's legal costs, which could be $40,000 to $50,000. "I would have been responsible if things turned out badly," Bev says. "I would have ruined the family." So she gave her siblings several chances to back down. They adamantly declined.

A Difficult Legal Battle

On May 17, 2001, after two years of legal wrangling, the trial began. Medical lawsuits are a nasty business. The plaintiffs need to prove, in effect, that a highly trained professional acted incompetently. The doctor, in turn, wants to save his reputation by blaming bad outcomes on someone, or something, else. The ugly stuff started right away. During his opening statement, Chin's defense attorney, Robert M. Slattery, insinuated that Bev had killed Bill Bergman when she gave him the final dose of morphine secured by the hospice nurse. The Bergman side gasped at the accusation.

As days turned into weeks, tensions in the courtroom grew. Says Bev, "I didn't like being on the stand. It felt like you were going through it all over again. And the attorney kept hammering on the same thing, trying to make you contradict yourself, trying to discredit you." Her sister, Alice, left the courtroom four or five times when

Chin and the medical-center nurses seemed to display callousness about her father's pain. "We weren't supposed to get emotional," Alice says, "but at some points we wanted to wring their necks."

The stress took its toll. Robert lost 15 to 20 pounds during the three-week trial; Bev lost 5. All of them—Geagan included—had trouble sleeping. "I had never had a case with more of an effect on public health," he says. "I thought, 'What if I try it and we lose? The message would be that you can undertreat the elderly for pain and it doesn't matter.'"

In their case, the Bergmans' lawyers charged that Chin was woefully underinformed about pain-management strategies. In fact, he admitted to no education on this subject beyond a pharmacology class in medical school 30 years ago and a lunchtime seminar more recently. The Bergmans also cast doubt on Chin's assertion that Bill Bergman had reacted negatively to the morphine given him in the emergency room: Chin had not noted this reaction on Bergman's chart or relayed it to the nurses. Further, expert witnesses said it was unlikely that Bev had hastened her dad's death. (Chin's lawyers were repeatedly contacted to comment on the story, but they did not return phone calls.)

Both sides rested their case and the jury adjourned. After four very long days of deliberation, they returned to the courtroom. Bev, Robert, Alice, and Alice's 26-year-old daughter, Jennifer, sat holding hands, waiting for the verdict. Although they were all terrified about the jury's decision, the three siblings had never felt closer. Says Bev, "I felt like my family had united to do the right thing." The jury agreed, finding for the Bergmans and awarding them $1.5 million, a sum that vastly exceeded their expectations. "It was kind of a sad victory because we really weren't trying to harm Dr. Chin," Bev says. "We didn't jump up and down, but we were glad."

The Precedent-Setting Decision

Even though the award was reduced to $250,000 (to comply with the elder-abuse statute limit), the decision was widely hailed as precedent-setting. "It demonstrated that the court considers adequate pain management a part of good medical practice," says David E. Joranson, director of the Pain and Policy Studies Group at the University of Wisconsin Medical School. The verdict has also encouraged doctors, perhaps nervous about their own pain-management practices, to sign up for pain-relief seminars. A few months after the trial's conclusion, California Governor Gray Davis signed a law that might ease the need for related lawsuits. Bev testified on behalf of this statute, which requires state doctors to undergo continuing education and calls on the Medical Board of California to track complaints about the mishandling of pain care by physicians—the first such law in the country.

After the trial, many people who had never met Bill Bergman told his kids that their father would have been proud of them. Their immediate reaction was to disagree. Says Bev: "At first I thought he would think I'm making too much of this, because he was so stoic." But after further reflection she changed her mind: "I think he would be happy for us, that we've done something to help other people. I think he would like that."

Physician-Assisted Suicide Is Ethical

Peter Rogatz

According to physician Peter Rogatz, legalization of physician-assisted suicide would offer significant humanitarian benefits. He argues that some terminally ill patients endure suffering that cannot be relieved by any available palliative methods and believes that such patients, although not numerous, should have the right to end their own suffering. He asserts that the physician who helps such a patient is performing a humanitarian and highly ethical act. He recognizes that critics fear the legalization of assisted suicide would lead down a slippery slope to unrestricted mercy killings, but the author asserts that appropriate controls and supervision can minimize the risk of abuse. A former professor of community and preventive medicine at the State University of New York at Stony Brook, Rogatz is a founding board member of the group Compassion in Dying of New York.

Physician-assisted suicide is among the most hotly debated bioethical issues of our time. Every reasonable person prefers that no patient ever contemplate suicide—with or without assistance—and recent improvements in pain management have begun to reduce the number of patients seeking such assistance. However, there are some patients who experience terrible suffering that cannot be relieved by any of the therapeutic or palliative techniques that medicine and nursing have to offer and some of those patients desperately seek deliverance.

This is not about physicians being killers. It's about patients whose suffering we can't relieve and about not turning away from them when they ask for help. Will there be physicians who feel they can't do this? Of course, and they shouldn't be obliged to. But if other physicians consider it merciful to help such patients by merely writing a prescription, it is unreasonable to place them in jeopardy of criminal prosecution, loss of license, or other penalty for doing so.

Many arguments are put forward for maintaining the prohibition against physician-assisted suicide, but I believe they are outweighed

Peter Rogatz, "The Positive Virtues of Physician-Assisted Suicide," *Humanist*, vol. 61, November/December 2001, pp. 31–34.

by two fundamental principles that support ending the prohibition: patient autonomy—the right to control one's own body—and the physician's duty to relieve suffering.

Society recognizes the competent patient's right to autonomy—to decide what will or won't be done to his or her body. There is almost universal agreement that a competent adult has the right to self-determination, including the right to have life-sustaining treatment withheld or withdrawn. Suicide, once illegal throughout the United States, is no longer illegal in any part of the country. Yet assisting a person to take her or his own life is prohibited in every state but Oregon. If patients seek such help, it is cruel to leave them to fend for themselves, weighing options that are both traumatic and uncertain, when humane assistance could be made available.

An Obligation to Relieve Suffering

The physician's obligations are many but, when cure is impossible and palliation has failed to achieve its objectives, there is always a residual obligation to relieve suffering. Ultimately, if the physician has exhausted all reasonable palliative measures, it is the patient—and only the patient—who can judge whether death is harmful or a good to be sought. Marcia Angell, former executive editor of the *New England Journal of Medicine*, has put it this way:

> The highest ethical imperative of doctors should be to provide care in whatever way best serves patients' interests, in accord with each patient's wishes, not with a theoretical commitment to preserve life no matter what the cost in suffering. . . . The greatest harm we can do is to consign a desperate patient to unbearable suffering—or force the patient to seek out a stranger like Dr. Kevorkian.

Let's examine the key arguments made against physician-assisted suicide. First, much weight is placed on the Hippocratic injunction to do no harm. It has been asserted that sanctioning physician-assisted suicide "would give doctors a license to kill," and physicians who accede to such requests have been branded by some as murderers. This is both illogical and inflammatory. Withdrawal of life-sustaining treatment—for example, disconnecting a ventilator at a patient's request—is accepted by society, yet this requires a more definitive act by a physician than prescribing a medication that a patient has requested and is free to take or not, as he or she sees fit. Why should the latter be perceived as doing harm when the former is not? Rather than characterizing this as "killing," we should see it as bringing the dying process to a merciful end. The physician who complies with a plea for final release from a patient facing death under unbearable conditions is doing good, not harm, and her or his actions are entirely consonant with the Hippocratic tradition.

Patients Trust Physicians to Help Them

Second, it is argued that requests for assisted suicide come largely from patients who haven't received adequate pain control or who are clinically depressed and haven't been properly diagnosed or treated. There is no question that proper management of such conditions would significantly reduce the number of patients who consider suicide; any sanctioning of assistance should be contingent upon prior management of pain and depression.

However, treatable pain is not the only reason, or even the most common reason, why patients seek to end their lives. Severe body wasting, intractable vomiting, urinary and bowel incontinence, immobility, and total dependence are recognized as more important than pain in the desire for hastened death. There is a growing awareness that loss of dignity and of those attributes that we associate particularly with being human are the factors that most commonly reduce patients to a state of unrelieved misery and desperation.

Third, it is argued that permitting physician-assisted suicide would undermine the sense of trust that patients have in their doctors. This is curious reasoning; patients are not lying in bed wondering if their physicians are going to kill them—and permitting assisted suicide shouldn't create such fears, since the act of administering a fatal dose would be solely within the control of the patient. Rather than undermining a patient's trust, I would expect the legalization of physician-assisted suicide to enhance that trust. I have spoken with a great many people who feel that they would like to be able to trust their physicians to provide such help in the event of unrelieved suffering—and making that possible would give such patients a greater sense of security. Furthermore, some patients have taken their own lives at a relatively early stage of terminal illness precisely because they feared that progressively increasing disability, without anyone to assist them, would rob them of this option at a later time when they were truly desperate. A patient contemplating suicide would be much less likely to take such a step if he or she were confident of receiving assistance in the future if so desired.

Fourth, it is argued that patients don't need assistance to commit suicide; they can manage it all by themselves. This seems both callous and unrealistic. Are patients to shoot themselves, jump from a window, starve themselves to death, or rig a pipe to the car exhaust? All of these methods have been used by patients in the final stages of desperation, but it is a hideous experience for both patient and survivors. Even patients who can't contemplate such traumatic acts and instead manage to hoard a supply of lethal drugs may be too weak to complete the process without help and therefore face a high risk of failure, with dreadful consequences for themselves and their families.

Fifth, it is argued that requests for assisted suicide are not frequent enough to warrant changing the law. Interestingly, some physicians say they have rarely, if ever, received such requests, while others say they have often received requests. This is a curious discrepancy, but I think it can be explained: the patient who seeks help with suicide will cautiously test a physician's receptivity to the idea and simply won't approach a physician who is unreceptive. Thus, there are two subsets of physicians in this situation: those who are open to the idea of assisted suicide and those who aren't. Patients are likely to seek help from the former but not from the latter.

A study carried out by the University of Washington School of Medicine queried 828 physicians (a 25 percent sample of primary care physicians and all physicians in selected medical subspecialties) with a response rate of 57 percent. Of these respondents, 12 percent reported receiving one or more explicit requests for assisted suicide, and one-fourth of the patients requesting such assistance received prescriptions.

A survey of physicians in San Francisco treating AIDS patients brought responses from half, and 53 percent of those respondents reported helping patients take their own lives by prescribing lethal doses of narcotics. Clearly, requests for assisted suicide can't be dismissed as rare occurrences.

Sixth, it is argued that sanctioning assisted suicide would fail to address the needs of patients who are incompetent. This is obviously true, since proposals for legalization specify that assistance be given only to a patient who is competent and who requests it. However, in essence, this argument says that, because we can't establish a procedure that will deal with every patient, we won't make assisted suicide available to any patient. What logic! Imagine the outcry if that logic were applied to a procedure such as organ transplantation, which has benefited so many people in this country.

Criteria for Granting Assisted Suicide

Seventh, it is argued that once we open the door to physician-assisted suicide we will find ourselves on a slippery slope leading to coercion and involuntary euthanasia of vulnerable patients. Why so? We have learned to grapple with many slippery slopes in medicine—such as Do Not Resuscitate (DNR) orders and the withdrawal of life support. We don't deal with those slippery slopes by prohibition but, rather, by adopting reasonable ground rules and setting appropriate limits.

The slippery slope argument discounts the real harm of failing to respond to the pleas of real people and considers only the potential harm that might be done to others at some future time and place. As in the case of other slippery slopes, theoretical future harm can be mitigated by establishing appropriate criteria that would have to be met before a patient could receive assistance. Such criteria have been outlined frequently. Stated briefly, they include:

1. The patient must have an incurable condition causing severe, unrelenting suffering.

2. The patient must understand his or her condition and prognosis, which must be verified by an independent second opinion.
3. All reasonable palliative measures must have been presented to and considered by the patient.
4. The patient must clearly and repeatedly request assistance in dying.
5. A psychiatric consultation must be held to establish if the patient is suffering from a treatable depression.
6. The prescribing physician, absent a close preexisting relationship (which would be ideal), must get to know the patient well enough to understand the reasons for her or his request.
7. No physician should be expected to violate his or her own basic values. A physician who is unwilling to assist the patient should facilitate transfer to another physician who would be prepared to do so.
8. All of the foregoing must be clearly documented.

Application of the above criteria would substantially reduce the risk of abuse but couldn't guarantee that abuse would never occur. We must recognize, however, that abuses occur today—in part because we tolerate covert action that is subject to no safeguards at all. A more open process would, in the words of philosopher and ethicist Margaret Battin, "prod us to develop much stronger protections for the kinds of choices about death we already make in what are often quite casual, cavalier ways."

It seems improbable that assisted suicide would pose a special danger to the elderly, infirm, and disabled. To paraphrase British economist John Maynard Keynes, in the long run we are all elderly, infirm, or disabled and, since society well knows this, serious attention would surely be given to adequate protections against abuse. It isn't my intention to dispose glibly of the fear that society would view vulnerable patients as a liability and would manipulate them to end their lives prematurely. Of course, this concern must be respected, but the risk can be minimized by applying the criteria listed above. Furthermore, this argument assumes that termination of life is invariably an evil against which we must protect vulnerable patients who are poor or otherwise lacking in societal support. But, by definition, we are speaking of patients who desperately wish final release from unrelieved suffering, and poor and vulnerable patients are least able to secure aid in dying if they want it. The well-to-do patient may, with some effort and some good luck, find a physician who is willing to provide covert help; the poor and disenfranchised rarely have access to such assistance in today's world.

Legal Euthanasia Will Not Be Abused

Eighth, it is argued that the Netherlands experience proves that societal tolerance of physician-assisted suicide leads to serious abuse. Aside from the fact that the data are subject to varying interpretation depending upon which analysis one believes, the situation in the Netherlands holds few lessons for us, because for many years that country followed the ambiguous practice of technically prohibiting but tacitly permitting assisted suicide and euthanasia.

The climate in the United States is different; our regulatory mechanisms would be different—much stricter, of course—and we should expect different outcomes. The experience of Oregon—the only one of our fifty states to permit physician-assisted suicide—is instructive. During the first three years that Oregon's law has been in effect, seventy terminally ill patients took advantage of the opportunity to self-administer medication to end protracted dying. Despite dire warnings, there was no precipitous rush by Oregonians to embrace assisted suicide. The poor and the uninsured weren't victimized; almost all of these seventy patients had health insurance, most were on hospice care, and most were people with at least some college education. There were no untoward complications. The Oregon experience is far more relevant for the United States than the Dutch experience, and it vindicates those who, despite extremely vocal opposition, advocated for the legislation.

Ninth, it has been argued that a society that doesn't assure all its citizens the right to basic health care and protect them against catastrophic health costs has no business considering physician-assisted suicide. I find this an astonishing argument. It says to every patient who seeks ultimate relief from severe suffering that his or her case won't be considered until all of us are assured basic health care and financial protection. These are certainly proper goals for any decent society, but they won't be attained in the United States until it becomes a more generous and responsible nation—and that day seems to be far off. Patients seeking deliverance from unrelieved suffering shouldn't be held hostage pending hoped-for future developments that are not even visible on the distant horizon.

The Status Quo Needs to Change

Finally, it is argued that the status quo is acceptable—that a patient who is determined to end his or her life can find a sympathetic physician who will provide the necessary prescription and that physicians are virtually never prosecuted for such acts. There are at least four reasons to reject the status quo. First, it forces patients and physicians to undertake a clandestine conspiracy to violate the law, thus compromising the integrity of patient, physician, and family. Second, such secret compacts, by their very nature, are subject to faulty implementation with a high risk of failure and consequent tragedy for both patient and family. Third, the assumption that a determined patient can find a sympathetic physician applies, at best, to middle- and upper-income persons who have ongoing relationships with their physicians; the poor, as I've already noted, rarely have such an opportunity. Fourth, covert action places a physician in danger of criminal prosecution or loss of license and, although such penalties are assumed to be unlikely, that risk certainly inhibits some physicians from doing what they believe is proper to help their patients.

I believe that removing the prohibition against physician assistance, rather than opening the flood gates to ill-advised suicides, is likely to reduce the incentive for suicide: patients who fear great suffering in the final stages of illness would have the assurance that help would be available if needed and they would be more inclined to test their own abilities to withstand the trials that lie ahead.

Physician-Assisted Suicide Is Humane

Life is the most precious gift of all, and no sane person wants to part with it, but there are some circumstances where life has lost its value. A competent person who has thoughtfully considered his or her own situation and finds that unrelieved suffering outweighs the value of continued life shouldn't have to starve to death or find other drastic and violent solutions when more merciful means exist. Those physicians who wish to fulfill what they perceive to be their humane responsibilities to their patients shouldn't be forced by legislative prohibition into covert actions.

There is no risk-free solution to these very sensitive problems. However, I believe that reasonable protections can be put in place that will minimize the risk of abuse and that the humanitarian benefits of legalizing physician-assisted suicide outweigh that risk. All physicians are bound by the injunction to do no harm, but we must recognize that harm may result not only from the commission of a wrongful act but also from the omission of an act of mercy. While not every physician will feel comfortable offering help in these tragic situations, many believe it is right to do so and our society should not criminalize such humanitarian acts.

Physician-Assisted Suicide Is Not Ethical

Wesley J. Smith

In the following selection, Wesley J. Smith argues that the legalization of physician-assisted suicide would lead to unethical practices and even outright murder. If physician-assisted suicide becomes widely accepted in the United States, he warns, doctors will gain the power to decide when it is time to end a patient's life, regardless of whether or not the patient wants to die. This situation already exists in the Netherlands, he contends, where legalized euthanasia has led to thousands of patients being killed without their consent. The author concludes that the sanctity of life for all people—whether dying, disabled, or elderly—should be upheld. Smith is an attorney for the Task Force on Euthanasia and Assisted Suicide and the author of *Culture of Death: The Assault on Medical Ethics in America.*

They call them "death angels"—doctors or other medical professionals who stalk hospital and nursing-home corridors searching quietly for the sickest and most defenseless patients to secretly dispatch. The term is most unfortunate, carrying with it the implication that these premeditated killers of sick, disabled, and dying people are somehow doing their victims a favor by "ending their suffering." In fact, there is nothing angelic about presuming the right to decide that the time has come for another human being to die.

Angels of Death

Lately, the United States has been experiencing something of a boom in so-called angels of death:

- In Los Angeles, former respiratory therapist Efren Saldivar has pleaded not guilty to charges that he murdered six elderly patients at Glendale Adventist Medical Center between December 1996 and August 1997. Salvidar told the police that he killed more than 50 patients, a confession he has since recanted. Twenty former patients' bodies were exhumed, providing the evidence upon which to charge Salvidar with murder. The alleged

Wesley J. Smith, "Culture of Death Angels," www.nationalreview.com, March 6, 2001.

serial killer is behind bars awaiting trial.

- In September 2000, in Uniondale, New York, former physician Michael Swango pleaded guilty to killing three patients at a Long Island Veterans hospital with injections that stopped their hearts. Before allegedly killing his victims, he had placed Do Not Resuscitate (DNR) orders on their medical charts to prevent medical personnel from performing CPR. Swango received a life sentence.
- In Oakland County, Michigan, where pathologist Jack Kevorkian used to play, hospice nurse Anne Nicolai, after "finding God," wrote an e-mail to her boyfriend confessing to having overdosed three of her elderly hospice patients with morphine. The body of one of her alleged victims, a woman who had Alzheimer's disease, was exhumed and the Oakland County Medical Examiner ruled the death a homicide.
- In September 2000, in Utah, a jury convicted psychiatrist Robert Allen Weitzel of two counts of second-degree felony manslaughter and three counts of negligent homicide, for the morphine overdoses patients received at a geriatric/psychiatric unit Weitzel ran at the Davis Hospital and Medical Center in Layton. Weitzel's conviction was later overturned and he is free on bail awaiting a new trial.
- In Springfield, Massachusetts, nurse Kristen H. Gilbert is charged with murdering four of her patients and attempting to murder three others at the Veterans Affairs Medical Center in Northampton. Gilbert is accused of injecting her patients with adrenalin to make their hearts race fatally out of control.

A "Culture of Death"

The seeming increase in the number of medical professionals accused of killing their patients in recent years may be a mere coincidence. Then again, it may be the beginning of a trend. This isn't idle speculation. The sanctity of human life is under as intense attack in this country as we have seen since those bad old days when the likes of Sen. John C. Calhoun promoted slavery as a positive good. Indeed, our country is currently steeped in a "culture of death" in which dying—and even killing—are promoted by bioethicists and assisted-suicide advocates as acceptable answers to the individual difficulties associated with serious illness and disability, the emotional and financial hardships sometimes generated by family care-giving responsibilities, and the "crisis" in health-care resources. We have actually gotten to the point where the predominate opinion in bioethics holds that people with a "lower" quality of life have less moral value than "normal adults."

These death-culture attitudes lead to actual medical policies that hurt real people. Most famously, Oregon has legalized assisted suicide where studies show that most who swallow prescribed poison do so in order not to "burden" their families. Meanwhile, beneath the media's radar, "futile care" protocols are being quietly implemented in hospitals across the country that arrogantly give doctors and ethics committees the right to refuse *wanted* life-extending treatment unilaterally if the doctor believes the patient's quality of life is insufficient to justify the cost of care. At the same time, cognitively disabled patients—both conscious and unconscious—are made to die slow deaths by dehydration in all 50 states by having their tube-supplied food and water withheld or withdrawn on the basis that their lives are no longer worth living. In such a cultural milieu, is it really surprising that some medical professionals would take the extra step of "mercy" killing dying, elderly, and disabled patients or that a few evil psychopaths would use "compassion" as a front for the fulfillment of their homicidal obsessions?

The Slippery Slope

We need only look to the Netherlands for proof that widespread acceptance of the culture of death leads inexorably to non-voluntary euthanasia. The Netherlands has permitted doctors to kill patients who volunteer to die since a court decision essentially decriminalized the practice in 1973. Since then, Dutch doctors have skied down the steepest of slippery slopes, normalizing medicalized killing in the process. Today, Dutch doctors lethally inject dying people who ask for it, chronically ill people who ask for it, disabled people who ask for it, depressed people who ask for it, and disabled babies whose parents ask for it.

More to the point of this essay, killing by Dutch doctors had not been limited to voluntary cases. Study after study of Dutch euthanasia have repeatedly demonstrated that more than one thousand people who have not asked to be killed receive lethal injections by their doctors each year. The practice is so common that the ever-rational Dutch have given non-voluntary killing a name: "termination without request or consent." The murders of tens of thousands of Dutch patients killed in the last 30 years without request or consent (for that is what such killings are considered technically under Dutch law) have led to only a handful of prosecutions, and no doctors have been jailed for the practice.

A case reported in 2001 in the *British Medical Journal News* illustrates vividly the license that country has given Dutch doctors to kill catastrophically ill and disabled patients—even if they have not asked for euthanasia. Dr. Wilfred van Oijen, a Dutch general practitioner, was recently found guilty of murdering a dying 84-year-old patient despite her statements that she did not wish to die. The doctor said he killed the comatose woman because she had bed sores and was soaked in urine. But bed sores can be mostly prevented through regular turning and a catheter will prevent an incontinent patient from soiling her linens. Despite this, Oijen was not penalized, because the Amsterdam court ruled that he had merely made an "error of judgment" while acting "honorably and according to his conscience" when he ended his patient's life. (So much for "choice.")

We have not yet become so accustomed to medicalized killing in the United States that we are willing to countenance murder in our hospital wards. But we are moving in that general direction. Unless we begin to reassert the sanctity and inherent value of all human lives—*most especially* of those among us who are dying, disabled, and elderly—we may soon find that patients who need our protection the most will find themselves increasingly in danger of being hustled into an early grave by the very professionals they counted upon to do them no harm.

The Ethical Concerns Behind Organ Donation

Helen Buttery

In the following article, Helen Buttery explores the ethical controversy surrounding organ donation. She explains that once a person's heart stops beating, the organs no longer receive oxygenated blood and quickly become unusable for transplantation. Therefore, Buttery reports, most organs are taken from individuals who have been declared brain dead but whose heart and lungs are still functioning. Some doctors and bioethicists argue that the concept of brain death is not a legitimate one, Buttery writes; they maintain that if a body's heart and lungs are working, then death cannot be ethically declared. These critics also contend that during surgery to harvest organs, "brain-dead" patients often show signs of pain, which suggests that the brain still has some awareness. However, the author states, others in the medical community assert that organ donors must meet specific criteria defining brain death. They point out that patients who are brain dead usually are placed on ventilators to keep their lungs functioning; without this artificial aid, the patient's body would soon die. Buttery has written for the Canadian magazines *Maclean's* and *Chatelaine*.

Children are not supposed to die before their parents. It's an unwritten rule that, as Diane Craig knows, can be broken. Her daughter, 11-year-old Sandrine, was killed when a truck ran a stop sign and hit her school bus in Dunrobin, a bedroom community west of Ottawa, Canada. When Craig arrived at the hospital, her daughter lay in bed without a bruise or scratch on her. "She looked just beautiful, so I thought she was in a coma, she's going to come out of it, she's fine," she remembers. Called into the doctor's office 18 hours after the accident, Craig was told Sandrine was "brain dead"—the term used when brain function is deemed to have ceased totally and irreversibly. Craig had to accept that her little girl was not coming back. As she lay in bed beside Sandrine listening to her breathing and heartbeat, she

Helen Buttery, "When Does Life End?" *Maclean's*, vol. 115, January 28, 2002, pp. 50–51.

thought, "We can't bury a beating heart and breathing lungs." She decided to donate her daughter's organs.

A Legitimate Definition of Death?

What happened soon after that left Craig shaken: she was introduced to her daughter's anesthetist. "If she's brain dead," she wondered, "why do they have to put her to sleep?" It is a question that plagues many minds in the medical community. What bothers them is that when a surgeon retrieves organs, the donor's blood pressure and heartbeat rate may increase—normally signs of pain awareness. In that case, the anesthetist gives a higher dose of medication. To some specialists, that contradicts the notion of death. "You cannot say somebody is dead," says Christopher Doig, a critical care physician in Calgary, "but give them an anesthetic."

In fact, in such cases "the brain is not completely dead," says Peter Bailey, president of the Canadian Neurological Society and a neurologist in Saint John, N.B. If it were there would be no blood pressure or heartbeat. Brain death, says Bailey, is a "difficult concept." Still, he is among the vast majority of neurologists who think the 30-year-old term is a legitimate concept of death. And that's a critically important consideration, since organ donation hinges on the concept of brain death.

Although almost 1,900 transplants took place in 2001, more than 3,500 Canadians languish in queues for organ transplants and 150 die each year waiting for the lifesaving operation. At the same time, a minority of doctors complain that the acceptance of brain death is a cop-out that allows those desperately needed organ donations to take place while avoiding ethical questions. The situation is the same in most industrialized countries, which generally equate brain death with death. Japan is an exception. There, brain death has been a hotly debated moral issue for more than 30 years, and surgeons have been prosecuted for undertaking transplants from patients in that condition. In North America, some critics of the status quo argue that brain death does not mean patients are actually dead. "I would regard patients in the state called brain death to be severely neurologically disabled, comatose and dying. I would argue they are still alive," says Alan Shewmon, a pediatric neurologist at the University of California at Los Angeles and a leading critic of the notion of brain death.

In addition, a number of doctors find the guidelines used to determine brain death problematic. Criteria for brain death include: irreversible coma, an absence of brain-stem reflexes—such as pupils not responding to light—and an inability to breathe independently. Yet the application of these guidelines can differ from one hospital to the next.

Defining Brain Death

While the abortion dispute ponders "when does life begin?", the brain death question is "when does life end?" In the vast majority of deaths, a person stops breathing and the heart stops beating, oxygenated blood no longer reaches the organs and they quickly become unfit for transplant. But with brain deaths—frequently the result of head injury and accounting for less than three per cent of all deaths—the comatose patient continues to breathe with the aid of a ventilator and the organs stay healthy. The ventilator, a machine that assists breathing by forcing oxygen into the lungs—and the bloodstream—through a tube placed down the trachea, came into widespread use during the polio epidemic in the 1950s. "It became feasible to sustain somebody in a state where they would otherwise physiologically die," says Dr. Paul Boiteau, an intensive care physician in Calgary and president of the 250-member Canadian Critical Care Society. Before ventilators, brain dead patients did not survive. "Technology," says Boiteau, "has pushed us into thinking of death in a different light."

In 1968, the same year as Canada's first heart transplant, a committee at Harvard Medical School was first to outline the criteria for brain death. Its stated purpose was to "define irreversible coma as a new criterion for death." It was redefining death, it said, because of controversies surrounding the development of organ transplant procedures and the use of ventilators. "The Harvard Committee didn't give any reason as to why irreversible coma should be equated with death," says Shewmon. "Everyone accepts it because it's convenient, but not because it's valid." This categorization tied brain death and organ donation together, defining for the first time a group of potential donors—patients considered dead but with their hearts continuing to beat. "One has to happen for the other to happen," says Kerry Bowman, a bioethicist at the University of Toronto who worked as a medical social worker in intensive care units for 10 years. He feels that families faced with seeing a loved one labelled brain dead are less content about the diagnosis than the medical community lets on.

Guidelines for Diagnosis

An article in the *Canadian Journal of Neurological Science* in 1999 introduced guidelines for the diagnosis of brain death. While it had been commonplace to use an electroencephalogram (EEG) to verify the absence of electrical activity in the brain to determine brain death, that was no longer required. Today, physicians can declare brain death with a series of bedside tests, the most important being one to determine if the patient can breathe independently of a ventilator.

Most neurologists are satisfied with current methods. But Doig, who considers current testing "too simplistic," wants brain X-rays showing "irrefutable evidence of cessation of brain function" to become mandatory for the diagnosis. Although the guidelines state that tests to determine irreversible coma, an absence of brainstem reflexes and an inability to breathe independently should be done twice, some hospitals repeat the tests only if the patient is to be an organ donor. In some cases, for instance, care has been withdrawn without the benefit of the second set of tests if the family has consented to the removal of treatment, including ventilation.

In any case, what the clinicians are determining is simply whether a patient has irreversible brain damage. "Whether you are going to count brain death as human death is the next step, but that is not what goes on in the clinic or hospital," says Margaret Lock, a medical anthropologist at McGill University in Montreal whose book *Twice Dead: Organ Transplants and the Reinvention of Death* was published in 2001.

Western society generally views the body and the brain as separate entities, with the brain defining what it means to be a person—"I think, therefore I am." When the brain is destroyed, machines "support the corpse," says Dr. Bryan Young, a neurologist in London, Ont., who helped draw up the 1999 guidelines. Brain death is considered a form of death, says Young, because "the patient will never have awareness, cognitive function or human qualities that we associate with personhood."

A Utilitarian Concept of Death

That definition recognizes death as a process. Technology has allowed modern physicians to extend the period of suspension between life and death. Yet society generally recognizes death as an instantaneous event—bang, you're dead. Shewmon thinks medical historians will look back on this debate and realize how utilitarian the concept of brain death was. "Brain death is driven not by a clear understanding of death," he says, "but by a need for organs." Shewmon does not accept that the definition of life depends on a functioning brain. "It's certainly a *sine qua non* for health," he says, "but not for life." As evidence, he cites his published study of 175 cases of brain dead patients who survived longer than a week, including some children who lived more than a year. Brain dead women have sustained fetuses for several months until they could be delivered by Caesarean section. Dr. Michael Brear, a general practitioner in Vancouver who agrees with Shewmon's analysis, calls the medical profession the "naked emperor" for accepting the "fabrication" of brain death.

"People draw the lines in different ways," says Lock. "But it is only in rare occasions that a decision has to be made whether somebody in a permanent irreversible state of consciousness, who is hooked up for months to a respirator, is alive or dead. Or, are they as good as dead and can be counted as dead because there is no hope of them coming back to life?" A resolution to the debate is unlikely, leaving those faced with a loved one declared brain dead struggling to come to grips with the concept. Even though Diane Craig believed her daughter was gone, she stayed with Sandrine until she was wheeled into the operating room for organ retrieval. "I couldn't leave her," Craig says. "She was still breathing."

Revealing Unethical Practices in the Funeral Industry

Julie Polter

According to Julie Polter, the bereaved can become easy targets for unscrupulous funeral homes eager to make a big profit. Polter warns that many funeral directors resort to "upselling," or exerting pressure on vulnerable survivors to spend more than they had originally planned. Grieving family members often end up paying as much as 400 percent over wholesale for caskets, urns, or gravestones, she reports. The recent surge in conglomerates has only worsened the situation, the author cautions; the large funeral chains typically charge 25 percent more than do small funeral homes. One way to remedy this problem, Polter suggests, is for clergy and other church officials—who are already experienced with comforting the griefstricken—to become more involved in funeral planning to help the bereaved avoid getting scammed. Polter is the associate editor of the Christian magazine *Sojourners*.

Cheryl Grossman and her husband used to laugh together about all the "rigmarole" that most funeral services involved. So when he died suddenly in October 1997, Cheryl knew that he would want the arrangements to be simple. Grossman, with a friend to support her, went to a funeral home to arrange a direct cremation. The funeral director kept "upselling," pressing her to consider more expensive alternatives.

"Had I not had a friend who went with me, and had I not had a firm resolve, I probably would have signed anything," she says. "To be manipulated in that way at that time was one of the most obscene things I'd ever experienced."

Cheryl Grossman's funeral home encounter is a common one. Not so common is how she took her experience to church—and how her church embraced it. Cheryl's Catholic parish, St. Catherine of Siena in Austin, Texas, has offered a diverse array of practical and pastoral supports to the grieving for some time. In 1999, Grossman and two other parishioners helped create a death and funeral resource booklet that gathers information on all applicable parish ministries and other area

Julie Polter, "We All Have to Die. But Does It Have to Cost So Much!?" *Sojourners*, vol. 29, May/June 2000, pp. 28–33.

resources in a convenient portable form. It includes specific information on affordable funeral options, planning sheets, and step-by-step advice for those dealing with a death in the family.

People Are Uninformed About Funerals

Such a booklet is a simple, straightforward thing, but not every church would know how to welcome it. Most American Christians, including clergy, are almost as comfortable talking about the practical, concrete details of funerals as they are talking about the practical, concrete details of sex. In other words, the topic doesn't come up much. And unlike sex, funeral planning isn't a hot topic outside of church either.

So most just-bereaved people find themselves completely unprepared for the confusing and usually expensive decisions that have to be made about the preparation and final destination of a loved one's body. The unscrupulous within the American funeral industry count on and exploit such ignorance and the vulnerability of the bereaved. They sell embalming (with full cosmetic makeover) as both desirable and necessary, a casket as more than a box, and seek to equate one's love for the dead as directly proportional to dollars spent. It is big business, worth $25 billion annually in the United States alone. A family member's funeral is one of the largest single purchases that many adults will make in their lifetime.

Many funeral home directors, crematorium owners, and commercial cemetery operators sincerely strive to serve their communities; many do not have profit as their only goal. Nonetheless, to be naive about the commercial realities of most "death care" services can lead to exploitation and additional heartbreak. The current American standard for funeral care is, in large part, a product of marketing. It is a sentimental, mass-produced packaging of "traditions" (many of which never were), aided by the general public's ignorance of actual legal requirements concerning dead bodies.

No one deserves to be ripped off, especially when they are grieving. And, as might be expected, those who are the most traumatized or have the least money to lose are often the most vulnerable. This is reason enough to learn about misleading and fraudulent funeral practices and what can be done to counteract them.

Of equal importance for Christians and other people of faith is reclaiming the cultural and spiritual experience and rituals of death and grieving. Of all people, believers should know that, to bumper-sticker it, Death Happens. The average person will be a mourner several times in his or her life, and eventually, the funeral guest of honor. Preparing for what is just another part of life does not have to be inherently morbid. Those who've dug into (no pun intended) the topic of caring for the dead and the grieving testify to rich opportunities for creativity, ministry, community, and deepened spirituality.

Says Grossman, "It's a paradox that end of life issues can generate so much life. But they do."

Funerals Are Often Overpriced

Of course a little rage is in order. In 1963 writer Jessica Mitford's informative and witty *The American Way of Death* exhumed the funeral industry's machinations to hyper-commercialize our grief and pain. Decades of education and activism have brought some reforms, but our culture's death phobia and the siren call of profit seem to keep many shady and exploitative funeral practices going strong.

The unsuspecting can still pay 400 percent or more over wholesale for a casket. Embalming is still promoted as a public health or legal requirement when most often it is not. There are still funeral homes, cemeteries, and other "death care" providers who make fraudulent claims that certain caskets or vaults will protect or preserve the body (ultimately none of them do). Some funeral directors still have sales pitches designed to subtly shame survivors into spending much more than they or the deceased intended.

Even the most honest traditional funeral home operators are overseeing businesses with bottom lines that require huge markups and the successful marketing of completely unnecessary services and accessories. An overabundance of funeral homes in most regions of the country only increases the pressure to produce a large profit on each funeral. Since the griefstricken are in no mood to haggle, the selection of caskets, urns, plots, and grave markers are often the ultimate impulse buy.

One real-life example: Bob Massey, along with his sister and grandfather, made the arrangements after Massey's father died suddenly at age 49. The Dallas funeral home staff who assisted them were helpful and low-key—the family sensed no high pressure sales pitch. Insurance covered the burial costs (with little left over). Bob didn't think much about it until a year later when he saw a *60 Minutes* segment on funeral rip-offs. The show cited a figure as an example of an inflated price for a traditional funeral. The Massey family had paid three times that much for a relatively simple service. Massey now suspects the funeral home of tailoring its pricing to the amount of his father's insurance policy.

Regulating Funeral Homes Is Difficult

Over the past decade, corporate buy-outs also have been bringing that special conglomerate magic to the funeral business. The large funeral chains such as Service Corporation International (SCI) and Stewart Enterprises Inc. have expanded rapidly by quietly purchasing smaller chains or family-owned funeral homes (as well as cemeteries, monument dealers, etc.). The big companies usually retain the names of the local funeral homes (for the all-important element of familiarity and trust), but introduce seminar-honed sales techniques and efficiencies of scale such as centralized embalming facilities and warehousing of coffins and other supplies. The savings go to stockholders, not the grieving: In some markets, large consolidator's funerals cost over 25 percent more than those done by other firms in the same area.

Despite their aggressive business savvy, these mega-undertakers aren't invincible—one of the top three, Canada-based Loewen, went bankrupt in 1999, and SCI recently has endured anti-trust actions, regulatory fines, and plummeting stock. But big chains are still in business, posing as your friendly neighborhood undertaker while offering an expensive McFuneral to assuage your grief.

In 1984 the Federal Trade Commission (FTC) established the Funeral Rule as a national standard for funeral home practices. The rule requires funeral homes to provide customers with price lists of goods and services and itemized statements of funeral costs. They must also provide accurate and current information about state legal requirements (or lack thereof) regarding embalming, cremation, and vaults. Many funeral homes comply with the Funeral Rule, but those who don't might not get caught anytime soon. The FTC is notoriously lax in enforcing the rule and has no mechanism in place to assess compliance. Most consumers don't even know the rule exists. *Modern Maturity* magazine reports that in a recent survey by the American Association of Retired Persons (AARP) "only 8 percent of those surveyed knew that funeral homes are required to provide customers with a general price list."

Another barrier to legal accountability is that the rule only applies to funeral homes, not other providers of related goods and services. "The lines blur with consolidation," says Lisa Carlson, director of the Funeral Consumers Alliance, which works for funeral industry reform. "Cemeteries and monument dealers sell caskets now." The Funeral Consumers Alliance, AARP, and other organizations are optimistic that they can get the FTC to bring cemeteries and monument and casket dealers under the rule. Then they can turn their attention to problems with prepay plans, "sealer caskets," and other industry angles geared to profit on our fear of death and on the vulnerability of the grieving.

Churches Need to Get Involved

Churches should be natural allies in such funeral advocacy work. But church response varies from place to place and congregation to congregation. For example, Catholic priests in some areas have started parish- or diocese-based affordable mortuary services and have emphasized bringing funerals back into the church. Conversely, in 1997 the Los Angeles Catholic archdiocese made a lease agreement with Stewart Enterprises Inc. (at the time the third largest funeral chain in the country), allowing the firm to build and operate upscale mortuaries in several of the archdioceses' cemeteries. While now nonsectarian, many of the nation's local memorial societies (nonprofit groups who cut funeral costs through cooperative buying power and are increasingly active for funeral reform and oversight) were formed under church leadership.

Most ministers work with the dying and grieving and officiate at funerals. But they don't necessarily know more than people in the pews about the ins and outs of funeral arrangements. The standard seminary education usually doesn't cover this level of nitty-gritty, nor do ministers usually accompany people to meetings with funeral home representatives.

"When a minister has to deal with a death in their own family, they are often shocked at the cost," says Terri Dalton, associate director of pastoral care and counseling for the East Ohio Conference of the United Methodist Church. "They have no idea it can be so high." Most pastors slowly learn the details of death and burial on the job. Some find a local funeral director they trust to guide them through the process.

The relationship between clergy and funeral homes can be good or bad for the person making funeral arrangements. "Unfortunately the funeral industry tries to network itself with many organizations that refer business to them. Their trade publications encourage volunteering with hospices, hospitals, and AIDS programs, for example," says Lamar Hankins, board president of the Funeral Consumers Alliance. Some funeral homes give donations to churches or gifts to clergy to encourage referrals. But, adds Hankins, "There are at least an equal number of clergy who are concerned about funeral industry excesses. They believe, as I do, that for people of faith, these things need to be returned more fully to the oversight of churches and religious groups."

"The churches can be the greatest allies of the funeral industry rip-off or they can be their biggest enemy," says Father Henry Wasielewski, a retired Catholic priest and Phoenix-based funeral activist. He believes that many clergy, especially those in wealthier churches, simply don't suspect anything amiss with the high costs of funerals. Others know there are problems but feel it would be too "political" to get involved; they'll find funds for the church member who can't afford a loved one's funeral, but not question why it costs so much. A few others happily take the golf club memberships or other freebies they get from the local funeral home.

Learning to Talk About Funerals

Wasielewski sees great potential for concerned clergy to do good, simply through disseminating information. "In my book, it's almost a social justice duty for pastors to find out if there's a local mortuary that charges less than others and to tell their people about it." This can get interesting, of course, if one or more funeral home directors belong to a congregation.

Not every pastor is eager to become a funeral crusader, and not just because of church politics. "Clergy are like other people—they are often really uncomfortable talking about death," says Dalton. "They don't necessarily want to bring up the topic of caskets, for instance." They are not alone. The spread of the hospice movement is evidence that American society slowly is becoming more open and knowledgeable about death and dying, but talking freely about funerals and burial arrangements is still often greeted with discomfort.

Lisa Carlson finds a certain irony in this. "It's as though we want to accompany the dying and then leap over the dead body to console the grieving."

Whether you are behind the pulpit or in the pew, there are practical and spiritual benefits to attending to the logistics, liturgy, and legalities of death.

There is not a single "smart buyer," correct and reverent way to hold a funeral. Culture, family situations, religious traditions, circumstances of death, and the practicalities of what is available in a given location all come to bear on the type of funeral a person or family might choose. For example, increasing numbers of Americans are choosing direct burial or cremation, with a memorial service afterward. But others, whether for theological or cultural reasons, aren't comfortable with these options. Fortunately, a wide range of funerals can be meaningful, fairly priced, and honoring to both God and the one who has died.

Getting Involved in Funeral Planning

But this takes preparation. The more entrepreneurial (or downright scamming) members of the funeral business have found ways to add outrageous mark-ups to the simplest of burial or cremation arrangements. You can't say no once you're dead, and your survivors may not have the strength or knowledge to do it for you. With preparation, it is possible to almost completely opt out of the system and have do-it-yourself funerals. If that's a bit much for your tastes, it's certainly not difficult to become informed and plan ahead for your own funeral.

The best life-out-of-death experiences happen when education and forethought come together with practical support from a community of faith. Some church people have found profound comfort and power in the work of caring for their own dead, including preparing and moving the body. Others don't want to even think about being that hands-on, but through a local memorial society or consortium of churches they've researched local funeral homes and found one with reasonable prices that's willing to negotiate a special group rate. Endless variations on these approaches are possible, depending on local resources and the unique gifts of your congregation.

Getting the word out on funeral planning and consumer rights can be a unique justice ministry for a church. "The communities that need this information the most are the ones that are least likely to have the financial and educational resources to stand the pressures of the funeral industry," says Cheryl Grossman. Means of outreach include printing up fact fliers, offering a funeral-planning workshop, or negotiating (and subsidizing?) affordable services with a willing local funeral home for those in your area who are struggling financially.

"You can't get out of life alive," someone once said. Spiritually speaking, Christians might not agree. But in physical terms, it sums it up nicely. Bodily death is an inevitable transition—not much choice in the matter. What the living can decide is whether that transition is one controlled overwhelmingly by commerce and the extremes of grief or one guided and supported within the community of the faithful.

Organizations to Contact

The editors have compiled the following list of organizations concerned with the issues presented in this book. The descriptions are derived from materials provided by the organizations. All have publications or information available for interested readers. The list was compiled on the date of publication of the present volume; the information provided here may change. Be aware that many organizations take several weeks or longer to respond to inquiries, so allow as much time as possible.

American Medical Association (AMA)
515 N. State St., Chicago, IL 60610
(312) 464-5000
website: www.ama-assn.org

Founded in 1847, the AMA is the primary professional association of physicians in the United States. It disseminates information concerning medical breakthroughs, medical and health legislation, educational standards for physicians, and other issues concerning medicine and health care. It opposes physician-assisted suicide. The AMA operates a library and offers many publications, including its weekly journal *JAMA*, the weekly newspaper *American Medical News*, and journals covering specific types of medical specialties.

American Society of Law, Medicine, and Ethics (ASLME)
765 Commonwealth Ave., Suite 1634, Boston, MA 02215
(617) 262-4990 • fax: (617) 437-7596
e-mail: info@aslme.org • website: www.aslme.org

The society's members include physicians, attorneys, health care administrators, and others interested in the relationship between law, medicine, and ethics. The organization has an information clearinghouse and a library, and it acts as a forum for discussion of issues such as euthanasia and assisted suicide. It publishes the quarterlies *American Journal of Law and Medicine* and *Journal of Law, Medicine, and Ethics*, the newsletter *ASLME Briefings*, and books such as *Legal and Ethical Aspects of Treating Critically and Terminally Ill Patients*.

Center for the Rights of the Terminally Ill (CRTI)
PO Box 54246, Hurst, TX 76054-2064
(817) 656-5143

CRTI is an educational, patient advocacy, and political action organization that opposes assisted suicide and euthanasia. Through education and legislative action, it works to ensure that the sick and dying receive professional, competent, and ethical health care. Its publications include pamphlets such as *Living Wills: Unnecessary, Counterproductive, Dangerous* and *Can Cancer Pain Be Relieved?*

Compassion in Dying
6312 SW Capitol Hwy., Suite 415, Portland, OR 97239
(503) 221-9556 • fax: (503) 228-9160
e-mail: info@compassionindying.org • website: www.compassionindying.org

Compassion in Dying provides information, counseling, and emotional support to terminally ill patients and their families, including information and counseling about intensive pain management, comfort or hospice care, and death-hastening methods. It promotes the view that terminally ill patients who seek to hasten their deaths should not have to die alone because their loved ones fear prosecution if they are found present. Compassion in Dying does not promote suicide but condones hastening death as a last resort when all other possibilities have been exhausted and when suffering is intolerable. It publishes the quarterly newsletter *Connections* and several pamphlets on intensive pain management and on coping with the death of a loved one.

Euthanasia Research and Guidance Organization (ERGO)
24829 Norris Ln., Junction City, OR 97448-9559
phone and fax: (541) 998-1873
e-mail: ergo@efn.org • website: www.finalexit.org

ERGO provides information and research findings on physician-assisted dying to persons who are terminally or hopelessly ill and wish to end their suffering. Its members counsel dying patients and develop ethical, psychological, and legal guidelines to help them and their physicians make life-ending decisions. The organization's publications include *Deciding to Die: What You Should Consider* and *Assisting a Patient to Die: A Guide for Physicians.*

Foundation of Thanatology
630 W. 168th St., New York, NY 10032
(212) 928-2066 • fax: (718) 549-7219 • fax: (914) 793-0813

This organization of health, theology, psychology, and social science professionals is devoted to scientific and humanist inquiries into death, loss, grief, and bereavement. The foundation coordinates professional, educational, and research programs concerned with mortality and grief. It publishes the periodicals *Advances in Thanatology* and *Archives of the Foundation of Thanatology*.

Funeral Consumers Alliance
PO Box 10, Hinesburg, VT 05461
(802) 482-3437
e-mail: info@funerals.org • website: www.funerals.org

The Funeral Consumers Alliance works to promote the affordability, dignity, and simplicity of funeral rites and memorial services. The alliance believes that every person should have the opportunity to choose the type of funeral or memorial service he or she desires. It provides information on body and organ donation and on funeral costs, and it lobbies for reform of funeral regulations at the state and federal levels. The alliance's publications include the end-of-life planning kit *Before I Go, You Should Know* and the quarterly *FCA Newsletter.*

The Hastings Center
21 Malcolm Gordon Rd., Garrison, NY 10524-5555
(845) 424-4040 • fax: (845) 424-4545
e-mail: mail@thehastingscenter.org • website: www.thehastingscenter.org

Since its founding in 1969, the center has played a central role in responding to advances in the medical, biological, and social sciences by raising ethical questions related to such advances. It conducts research and provides consultations on ethical issues such as assisted suicide and offers a forum for exploration and debate. The center publishes books, papers, guidelines, and the bimonthly *Hastings Center Report.*

The Hemlock Society
PO Box 101810, Denver, CO 80250-1810
(877) 436-5625 • fax: (303) 639-1224
e-mail: hemlock@hemlock.org • website: www.hemlock.org

The society believes that terminally ill individuals have the right to commit suicide. It supports the practice of voluntary suicide and physician-assisted suicide for the terminally ill. The society publishes books on suicide, death, and dying, including *Final Exit*, a guide for those suffering with terminal illnesses and considering suicide. Other publications include the pamphlet *Choosing a Hastened Death and Mental Health: Facts and Myths*, the videotape *A Gentle Ending*, and the quarterly newsletter *TimeLines*.

Human Life International (HLI)
4 Family Life Ln., Front Royal, VA 22630
(540) 635-7884 • fax: (540) 636-7363
e-mail: hli@hli.org • website: www.humanlifeinternational.org

HLI categorically rejects euthanasia and believes assisted suicide is morally unacceptable. The organization defends the rights of the unborn, the disabled, and those threatened by euthanasia. It provides education, advocacy, and support services. HLI's publications include the monthly newsletter *HLI Reports* and the booklet *Imposed Death: What You Need to Know About Mercy Killing and Assisted Suicide*.

International Association for Near-Death Studies (IANDS)
PO Box 502, E. Windsor Hill, CT 06028-0502
(860) 644-5216 • fax: (860) 644-5759
e-mail: office@iands.org • website: www.iands.org

IANDS is a worldwide organization of scientists, scholars, and others who are interested in or who have had near-death experiences. It supports the scientific study of near-death experiences and their implications, fosters communication among researchers on this topic, and sponsors support groups in which people can discuss their near-death experiences. The association publishes the quarterly newsletter *Vital Signs* and the annual *Journal of Near-Death Studies*.

International Task Force on Euthanasia and Assisted Suicide
PO Box 760, Steubenville, OH 43952
(740) 282-3810
website: www.internationaltaskforce.org

The task force opposes assisted suicide and euthanasia and strives to combat attitudes, programs, and policies that its members believe threaten the lives of those who are medically vulnerable. It supports the rights of people with disabilities and advocates the improvement of pain control for the seriously or terminally ill. The task force conducts seminars and workshops on euthanasia and related end-of-life issues. Its publications include pamphlets such as *Assisted Suicide: The Continuing Debate*, the book *Power over Pain: How to Get the Pain Control You Need*, and the periodic newsletter *Update*.

Living Bank
PO Box 6725, Houston, TX 77265
(800) 528-2971
e-mail: info@livingbank.org • website: www.livingbank.org

The bank is an international registry and referral service for people wishing to donate organs and/or tissue for transplantation, therapy, or research. Its volunteers speak to civic organizations about the benefits of organ donation, and its 350,000 donor population spreads through fifty states and sixty-three foreign countries. It provides educational materials on organ donation and publishes two newsletters, the quarterly *Bank Account* and the bimonthly *Living Banker*.

National Hospice and Palliative Care Organization (NHPCO)
1700 Diagonal Rd., Suite 625, Alexandria, VA 22314
(703) 837-1500 • fax: (703) 837-1233
e-mail: info@nhpco.org • website: www.nhpco.org

The NHPCO (originally the National Hospice Organization) was founded in 1978 to educate the public about the benefits of hospice care for the terminally ill and their families. It seeks to promote the idea that with the proper care and pain medication, the terminally ill can live out their lives comfortably and in the company of their families. The organization opposes euthanasia and assisted suicide. It conducts educational and training programs for administrators and caregivers in numerous aspects of hospice care. The NHPCO publishes grief and bereavement guides, brochures such as *Hospice Care: A Consumer's Guide to Selecting a Hospice Program* and *Communicating Your End-of-Life Wishes*, and the book *Hospice Care: A Celebration*.

Partnership for Caring (PFC)
1620 Eye St. NW, Suite 202, Washington, DC 20006
(202) 296-8071 • hotline: (800) 989-9455 • fax: (202) 296-8352
e-mail: pfc@partnershipforcaring.org • website: www.partnershipforcaring.org

Partnership for Caring is dedicated to improving treatment of the dying and to fostering communication about complex end-of-life decisions. The organization invented living wills in 1967 and operates the only national crisis and informational hotline dealing with end-of-life issues. PFC also provides educational materials for health care professionals and the general public, monitors state and federal legislation and court cases related to end-of-life care, and maintains a collaborative network with other organizations and individuals concerned with improving end-of-life care. Its publications include the article "Debunking the Myths of Hospice," the fact sheet "Women and End-of-Life Decisions," and the newsletter *Voices*.

Bibliography

Books

Rebecca Abrams	*When Parents Die: Learning to Live with the Loss of a Parent.* New York: Routledge, 1999.
David Barnard et al.	*Crossing Over: Narratives of Palliative Care.* New York: Oxford University Press, 2000.
Pauline Boss	*Ambiguous Loss: Learning to Live with Unresolved Grief.* Cambridge, MA: Harvard University Press, 1999.
Alexander A. Bove Jr.	*The Complete Book of Wills, Estates, and Trusts.* New York: Henry Holt, 2000.
Kathryn L. Braun, James H. Pietsch, and Patricia L. Blanchette, eds.	*Cultural Issues in End-of-Life Decision Making.* Thousand Oaks, CA: Sage, 2000.
John D. Canine	*What Am I Going to Do with Myself When I Die?* Stamford, CT: Appleton & Lange, 1999.
Grace Hyslop Christ	*Healing Children's Grief: Surviving a Parent's Death from Cancer.* New York: Oxford University Press, 2000.
Mark Cobb	*The Dying Soul: Spiritual Care at the End of Life.* Philadelphia: Open University Press, 2001.
Raphael Cohen-Almagor	*The Right to Die with Dignity: An Argument in Ethics, Medicine, and Law.* New Brunswick, NJ: Rutgers University Press, 2001.
Hannah Cooke	*When Someone Dies: A Practical Guide to Holistic Care at the End of Life.* Boston: Butterworth-Heinemann, 2000.
Kenneth J. Doka and Joyce D. Davidson, eds.	*Living with Grief: Who We Are, How We Grieve.* Washington, DC: Hospice Foundation of America, 1998.
David L. Edwards	*After Death? Past Beliefs and Real Possibilities.* London: Cassell, 1999.
Paul Edwards	*Reincarnation: A Critical Examination.* Amherst, NY: Prometheus Books, 2002.
Abdullah Fatteh and Naaz Fatteh	*At Journey's End: The Complete Guide to Funerals and Funeral Planning.* Los Angeles: Health Information Press, 1999.
John Hardwig	*Is There a Duty to Die? And Other Essays in Bioethics.* New York: Routledge, 2000.
Donald Heinz	*The Last Passage: Recovering a Death of Our Own.* New York: Oxford University Press, 1999.
Brian Innes	*Death and the Afterlife.* New York: St. Martin's Press, 1999.

Kenneth V. Iserson — *Grave Words: Notifying Survivors About Sudden, Unexpected Deaths*. Tucson, AZ: Galen Press, 1999.

Michael Kearney — *A Place of Healing: Working with Suffering in Living and Dying*. New York: Oxford University Press, 2000.

Ralph L. Klicker — *A Student Dies, a School Mourns: Dealing with Death and Loss in the School Community*. Philadelphia: Accelerated Development, 2000.

Loretta M. Kopelman and Kenneth A. De Ville, eds. — *Physician-Assisted Suicide: What Are the Issues?* Boston: Kluwer Academic, 2001.

Elisabeth Kübler-Ross — *On Death and Dying*. New York: Macmillan, 1969.

Elisabeth Kübler-Ross — *The Tunnel and the Light: Essential Insights on Living and Dying*. New York: Marlowe, 1999.

Myra MacPherson — *She Came to Live Out Loud: An Inspiring Family Journey Through Illness, Loss, and Grief*. New York: Scribner, 1999.

Julia Neuberger — *Dying Well: A Guide to Enabling a Good Death*. Cheshire, UK: Hochland & Hochland, 1999.

Richard John Neuhaus, ed. — *The Eternal Pity: Reflections on Dying*. Notre Dame, IN: University of Notre Dame Press, 2000.

Robert S. Olick — *Taking Advance Directives Seriously: Prospective Autonomy and Decisions Near the End of Life*. Washington, DC: Georgetown University Press, 2001.

Cynthia Pearson and Margaret L. Stubbs — *Parting Company: Understanding the Loss of a Loved One: The Caregiver's Journey*. Seattle: Seal Press, 1999.

Timothy E. Quill — *Caring for Patients at the End of Life: Facing an Uncertain Future Together*. New York: Oxford University Press, 2001.

Gordon Riches and Pam Dawson — *An Intimate Loneliness: Supporting Bereaved Parents and Siblings*. Philadelphia: Open University Press, 2000.

Kenneth Ring and Evelyn Elsaesser Valarino — *Lessons from the Light: What We Can Learn from the Near-Death Experience*. Portsmouth, NH: Moment Point Press, 2000.

Phyllis Rolfe Silverman — *Never Too Young to Know: Death in Children's Lives*. New York: Oxford University Press, 2000.

Margaret A. Somerville — *Death Talk: The Case Against Euthanasia and Physician-Assisted Suicide*. Montreal: McGill-Queen's University Press, 2001.

James Van Praagh — *Healing Grief: Reclaiming Life After Any Loss*. New York: Dutton, 2000.

Tony Walter — *On Bereavement: The Culture of Grief*. Philadelphia: Open University Press, 1999.

Lisa Yount — *Physician-Assisted Suicide and Euthanasia*. New York: Facts On File, 2000.

Marjorie B. Zucker, ed. — *The Right to Die Debate: A Documentary History*. Westport, CT: Greenwood Press, 1999.

Periodicals

Carl Becker — "The Meaning of Near-Death Experiences," *World & I*, March 1998. Available from 3600 New York Ave. NE, Washington, DC 20002.

Joel C. Berman — "We Should Let Dying Patients Write Their Own Final Scene," *Medical Economics*, January 13, 1997. Available from Five Paragon Dr., Montvale, NJ 07645-1742.

Jane Bernstein and Nichol Nelson — "Consoling Lessons," *Self*, March 2002. Available from PO Box 55470, Boulder, CO 80322.

Bill Beuttler — "Mourning in America," *Boston Magazine*, November 2001. Available from 300 Massachusetts Ave., Boston, MA 02115.

Consumer Reports on Health — "When to Ask About Hospice," January 2002. Available from PO Box 56355, Boulder, CO 80322.

Andrew J. DeMaio — "Drafting an Advance Directive for Health Care: Personal Reflections," *Estate Planning*, August 2002. Available from 395 Hudson St., 4th Fl., New York, NY 10014.

Peter Fenwick — "Living to Tell the Tale," *UNESCO Courier*, March 1998.

Amy L. Florian — "A Healing Society: May the Isolation of Grief Be Banished and the Bereaved Be Healed," *America*, July 1, 2000.

Neil Genzlinger — "On Death, Life's Cruelest Lesson," *New York Times*, September 15, 2002.

Jerome Groopman — "Dying Words," *New Yorker*, October 28, 2002.

Martin Gunderson and David J. Mayo — "Restricting Physician-Assisted Death to the Terminally Ill," *Hastings Center Report*, November 2000.

Amy Haddad — "Ethics in Action: Honoring a Daughter's Wish to Donate Her Organs," *RN*, May 2002. Available from Five Paragon Dr., Montvale, NJ 07645-1742.

Brendan I. Koerner — "Is There Life After Death?" *U.S. News & World Report*, March 31, 1997.

Mark S. Lachs and Pamela Boyer — "Have This Discussion Now: 'My Mom's Friends Say She Should Make Out an Advance Directive. What Is That, and Does She Really Need to Have It?'" *Prevention*, March 2002.

Kathryn Jean Lopez — "Dr. Death Down Under," *Human Life Review*, Fall 2001. Available from 150 E. 35th St., New York, NY 10016.

Peter W. Marty — "A Different Kind of Funeral," *Christian Century*, October 17, 2001.

Patty McCarty — "It's Getting Harder to Die," *National Catholic Reporter*, April 2, 1999. Available from PO Box 419281, Kansas City, MO 64141.

Lisa Miller "Why We Need Heaven," *Newsweek*, August 12, 2002.

Joshua Mitteldorf "Whence Comes Death?" *Humanist*, January/February 2002.

National Right to Life News "The Growing Trend Toward Involuntary Euthanasia," February 2001. Available from 512 10th St. NW, Washington, DC 20004-1401.

Anna Quindlen "On Losing Your Mom," *Good Housekeeping*, February 1998.

Andrea E. Richardson "Death with Dignity: The Ultimate Human Right?" *Humanist*, July/August 2002.

Emma Richler "Two or Three Things I Know About Grief," *Maclean's*, June 24, 2002.

Alexandra Robbins "When Your Mother Dies," *Cosmopolitan*, May 2002.

Thomas A. Shannon "Killing Them Softly with Kindness," *America*, October 15, 2001.

Rami Shapiro "Death and What's Next," *Tikkun*, July/August 1998.

Myles N. Sheehan "On Dying Well," *America*, July 29, 2000.

Peter Singer "Freedom and the Right to Die," *Free Inquiry*, Spring 2002. Available from Council for Secular Humanism, Box 5, Central Park Station, Buffalo, NY 14215.

Wesley J. Smith "The Birth of Hospice," *Human Life Review*, Fall 2001.

Bill Stieg and Lisa Jones "The Final Act: When It's Curtains, Don't Get Ripped Off," *Men's Health*, March 2002.

Judith Timson "Death Be Not Humble: Whatever Became of Simple Funerals?" *Chatelaine*, September 2002. Available from 777 Bay St., 9th Fl., Toronto, Ontario, M5W 1A7 Canada.

Tufts University Health and Nutrition Letter "Making End-of-Life Medical Decisions Ahead of Time," September 2002. Available from 53 Park Pl., 8th Fl., New York, NY 10007.

Wendy Murray Zoba "Dying in Peace," *Christianity Today*, October 22, 2001.

INDEX